Tell it as it was

Tell it as it Was

by Kathleen Hann

Writers Club Press

San Jose New York Lincoln Shanghai

Tell it as it Was

Writers Club Press
an imprint of iUniverse, Inc.

For information address:
iUniverse, Inc.
5220 S. 16th St., Suite 200
Lincoln, NE 68512
www.iuniverse.com

ISBN: 0-595-22790-2

Printed in the United States of America

For Peter

If you wish to be a writer and to move the hearts of men
To make the sad heart lighter by the magic of your pen,
Keep on writing, never falter, never cherish fear or doubt,
For the views of men will alter
And success will find you out.
—*Anon.*

Contents

Acknowledgements

I would like to thank my husband, Peter William Hann, for all his help and patience when I got uptight and there didn't seem any point in carrying on writing. I especially would like to thank him for being there and loving me for more than fifty years, and for having comfortable shoulders for me to cry on. We both know that when I see my name on the cover of a book, those shoulders will be put into use again!

I would like to thank the three computer experts in my family, my grandson, Peter and James Harris and their dad David. All three come to me rescue and tell me to calm down and that the computer isn't going to blow up when I press a wrong key. I especially like the wisdom of eighteen-year-old James who says that I helped him to understand many things when he was small, and it's his turn to help me now. *Nice one, James—thanks!*

Last and certainly not least, I would like to thank Dr Charles Muller for his great help and patience, especially in making sure that I was happy with each process before moving on. I really wish that there had been teachers like Dr Muller in the Black Country when I was a child.

Kathleen Hann

Introduction

Only at the twilight of our lives can we go right back to the beginning.

This is a good time for Peter and I, for after working many, many years in soul-destroying jobs, we are now both retired.

We have three marvellous children, four lovely grandchildren, and two beautiful baby great-grandsons; and I'm pleased to say all of our family live within walking distance from us. We have lots of good friends we meet regularly for outings, walking and eating out with. We have a busy, happy and comfortable lifestyle, and it was a great feeling of relief finally to pay off the mortgage on our three-bedroom bungalow—to know that it's ours, at last, down to the last brick!

From our window I can see Shropshire's most famous landscape—the beautiful Wrekin Hill.

There are playing fields from our back gate. At the moment there's a football match going on. I can hear the men shouting encouragement to each other and sometimes a swear word rips the air when one side gets the better of the other.

We have a lovely large garden which is our little bit of Heaven, a haven we believed to be ours when we bought the bungalow but which, in reality, belongs to the many different kinds of birds that live in our garden. Peter is the one with the "green fingers," for it's his tender loving care that's made the garden a haven of loveliness for all of us, birds included. I just sit on the swinging hammock remembering, reading, writing, or just idly watching the flowers grow. Sometimes I sit in the garden with our grandchildren and watch the many birds I put food out for. The bluetits have started to build their nest in the box I've provided for them. I've written on the box: "To let—apply within." They've taken up my offer and the rent they pay is the pleasure we derive watching them teach their chicks to fly.

There are eight magpies, one of whom we call "Fat Fred," for he is clearly the leader. When I put food on the bird table the magpies swoop down to inspect the offerings, but they never touch the food until "Fat Fred" has had his fill; only then can the others have their share. Magpies are very intelligent birds and fascinating to watch.

The garden goes up to a point. To one side is an old pit mound: after more than two hundred years nature has been kind to it, for now it's covered in gorse and beautiful trees. There's a great deal of wild life up there, for we hear owls hooting and foxes barking at night. There's a woodpecker and squirrels. Two of the squirrels—"Albert and Annie," as we call them—venture into the garden.

The fields go on for about three miles and then open to the most wonderful sight—our beautiful Wrekin Hill. When our grandchildren were very small they called it Grandma's Wrekin. Because I loved the Hill so much they believed it belonged to me. To me, the Wrekin means home.

It's where I belong.

My roots are in the Black Country, although now I'm beginning to wonder if they really are.

Two hundred years ago Coalbrookdale and the surrounding districts were a thriving area. It was the beginning of the Industrial Revolution, but when the area had been worked out and all the jobs disappeared, many people drifted away—many to make their way to the Black Country where there was plenty of work in the new chain, leather, nail, nut, and bolt businesses. I really believe my ancestors were amongst those people, for when we moved to Shropshire, every fibre of my being told me that I had finally come home!

My daughters were mature students and once I had the opportunity to attend an open day at a university with them. A highly educated middle-class lady historian spoke at great length about working-class women in the Nineteen Thirties.

I realise historians have to get their facts and figures right and study their subject for months, perhaps even years, for they have to write the truth as they see it; and yet, to me, that woman seemed so very cold and clinical. She spoke of Mrs A and Mrs B, and of how twenty per cent of women did one thing and thirty per cent did another thing, and so on…I was angry and pained at the way my mother's and grand-mother's lives had been reduced to statistics. I got up to speak, but my anger and pain got in the way. I know that I stumbled, and cried!

My Black Country accent is more pronounced when I'm upset. I wanted to say I really believe working-class history should be written by working-class people, that it was *our* past she spoke so coldly and matter-of-factly about. She may have had all the official details right, but I really wished I had the clearness of mind when standing up in that hall full of young women to tell that historian that history is about *more* than facts and figures—it's about *people. Real* people.

It's about pain, hurt, hunger, disappointment, humiliation, but most of all it's about the utter frustration of living (no, not living, *existing*) from one pay day to another—the never, never ending slog of the treadmill.

I could get all the facts and figures of the "Black Hole of Calcutta" and write then all down, but I couldn't write about it with great feeling and depth because I wasn't there. But I can and will write with feeling and compassion about the Black Country working-class people of the thirties—because that was where I spent my short childhood.

Although it has often been painful for me to remember, and many, many times my tears have smudged the pages when putting pen to paper, I have wiped my eyes and started again.

I will write the way I feel.

This is my style….

This is *me*….

We now have a comfortable and happy lifestyle and hopefully we will never again in our lives have to worry about money, or live from one payday to the next. My Black Country roots taught me some very hard lessons I shall never forget, and I'm grateful for them. Life is very good to us now, but it wasn't always that way.

Thank goodness I was much too young to realise the anguish, pain and heartache my mother had to suffer to decently raise her family during the depression, and to survive the means test of the nineteen thirties.

My story is dedicated to two women, first and foremost to my mother who taught me so much. She was the very best teacher I ever had. She taught me survival, she taught me that family is all-important; but most of all, she taught me love and compassion. Like me, she left school at the age of fourteen. She had very little education, but had more commonsense in her little finger than lots of people have in their whole bodies.

My thanks and dedication must also go to the lady historian, who shall remain nameless except to me and my daughters, for she was the one who made me so angry—so angry in fact that I felt inspired to write this book, fired with the urge to explain about those times. I went straight home after listening to her and started to write, and carried on writing throughout the night. Pages and pages were covered, but the most weird and really frightening thing is that when I re-read what I had written it seemed like someone else had written down the information—for there were things there I didn't realise I knew about. I must have pulled all that information right from my sub-conscious mind. It was information that had lain dormant for so many years. It was so very strange and scary that I didn't have any sleep that night. As soon as it was morning I phoned my elder sister and asked her about those things, and she confirmed everything I had written down. I had never seen the inside of a university before. It had always been my impossible and unheard-of dream to go to university; yet the magic and beauty of the creative process got to me and I really wanted to explain and get through to all those young girls about the hardship of life in the thirties.

After my stumbling attempt of speaking at that seminar I sat down to a deafening silence. I wanted the floor to open and swallow me up. But then there was a loud noise, and I turned around to see all those students standing up and clapping!

It took some time to realise the applause was for me!

They all came to shake my hand and each one made the same remark: "Tell it as it was!"

At that seminar I was mostly angry with myself for not having the confidence or the experience to say all the many things I wanted to say. The lady historian made me determined to somehow try to find the right words to convey the hopelessness, the utter despair of the working-class Black Country during those terrible times.

This is my Social History…

It will never get me a degree or even an O-level. But that's not important now, although there was a time when it would have meant so much to me.

My Social History taught me some very hard lessons I could never have been taught at any university, and which the historian, for all her education, will never, never comprehend.

1

"**R**un upstairs and see the new baby doll your mom has got for you!"

My dad smiled as he made this announcement to Jessie, my sister who was then only six. She ran up those old rickety stairs only to be very disappointed to find it wasn't a baby doll at all—it was just another baby.

I was the seventh of my parents' eight children, and was born January 26, 1930, on my parents' twelfth wedding anniversary.

I was christened Kathleen.

I wasn't much of an anniversary present for birth control was virtually unknown by the working class at that time; indeed, it was withheld from them by the current government which needed factory and bullet fodder for the future. It certainly wasn't considered important in high places that poor people kept producing children they couldn't afford to keep, that women were absolutely terrified every month in case they were pregnant, and that when they found they were, they suffered awful sleepless nights and terrible anguish through worrying about how on earth they were going to manage to feed another mouth without the rest of the children going without.

My mother lost her first two babies when they were only a few days old. I find it impossible to imagine the great sense of loss she must have felt. Her next two babies both had pneumonia at different times. In those days before penicillin, pneumonia was considered a life or death situation. The babies had to be nursed night and day for twenty-one days; after that time they either recovered or died. Those three weeks were called the crisis time. My mom wrapped her babies in cotton wool: each day she would remove a piece of the cotton wool. Thankfully my elder brother Eric and elder sister Jessie both recovered, thanks to my mom's careful nursing.

Next came my brother Bernard. The baby before me died at the age of eighteen months, while my younger sister Margaret was born three years after me.

Mom must have used grandma's bedroom to have her confinements. We lived in a two-up two-down, back-to-back terraced house. Grandma had one bedroom while the other was shared between us five children; there were two double beds in that room—one for my two brothers, and one for my two sisters and I.

There was a rope strung high across the middle of the room. Mom had draped old curtains and worn-out blankets across the line to give us some small privacy. We could talk through the curtains and my brothers would tell us jokes and stories, but none of us were allowed to move the curtain or cross that line except to go in and out of the room.

Mom and dad slept in the tiny living room. I don't know how they slept for I certainly don't remember any bed or comfort down there. Fortunately for me, I don't remember much at all of that first home. I know the houses had once belonged to the fire brigade and that they were very old and dilapidated. The rent was four shillings a week. I remember Mr Ward, the fire station officer, who was a very kind man: he used to buy ice creams for all the children in the yard and gave us rides on the fire engine. He pretended to pull pennies from our ears and he would then give us the pennies. He didn't have any children of his own.

My sister Margaret was born when I was three years old, and I've been told I was very jealous of her—so much, in fact, that I sat at the bottom of mom's bed pulling faces at mom and the baby. I must have been making really awful faces for my jaw locked and my face went all lop-sided. My mom screamed for help and the next-door neighbour came running in, looked at my distorted face and immediately gave me an almighty punch on the side of my jaw. It made an awful loud noise as it clicked back into place!

One neighbour was shunned by most of the women. It was years later before I realised why: she was an unmarried mother and it appears she had several children, all with different fathers. In those days the majority of people looked down on unmarried mothers, but she and my mom became good friends, helping each other out at their confinements.

At the back of the houses was the old brew house that had to be shared by four families, each woman having to take her turn doing her washing on different days. There was only a cold-water tap with an old boiler that had to be stoked up every day. I doubt very much if that boiler ever went cold, four large families regularly having to use it. Washing was an all-day job with the boiling, scrubbing, then swilling. The hardest job was turning the mangle to rinse the water out of the clothes; after all that work the maiding tub would be emptied into the yard which would then be swilled down with the soapy water.

The one toilet at the back of the houses was also shared. It was terrible if you were in a hurry to use it, especially if one of the men had been smoking dog ends (the bits of tobacco saved from used cigarettes and then re-rolled). The smell would be awful! Each person had to take their own piece of newspaper with them. There were no luxuries like toilet paper in those days, and even if there had been we wouldn't have been able to afford any. I recall one boy being rushed to hospital because he had used paper from a magazine that still had a metal clip in it; the clip had wedged into his backside and he had to have an operation to remove it. The teasing he received from everyone by far outweighed the pain he suffered.

It was an ongoing struggle for my mom—cleaning, polishing, scrubbing, and generally trying to make that house a fit place to bring her children up in. It was a losing battle right from the start for it was a very old house. There were bugs in the brickwork. Although I only spent the first five years of my life in that house, I can still remember the fleas which would wake us up and how we found big red bite-marks all over us; but most of all I remember the sweet awful sickly smell of the bugs. The memory of that smell will remain with me forever. It must have been sheer hell for my mom to raise her family in those conditions, for she regarded cleanliness next to godliness.

We were on Parish relief which meant, simply, that there wasn't enough money to live on. Someone from the council would come to inspect the house to see if there was anything of value, and if there was it had to be sold. People were only allowed the very bare essentials to live on. What the people from the parish didn't realise with all their great wisdom was that people had already sold any valuables they had ever possessed, and that only when they had reached rock bottom and hadn't enough money to feed their children would they finally go cap in hand to the parish. If anyone had a cat or dog they were told the pet had to go because keeping it would mean another mouth to feed. People would take their pets round to their neighbours while the people from the parish were inspecting their homes.

My mom was a very proud lady. It must have given her great distress to have to ask for charity. I truly believe she would have starved rather than ask for help for herself, but she had to swallow her pride for the sake of her children. That thought angers me still. My mom had long sold the only thing of value she had, which was her wedding ring. She wore a penny curtain ring from Woolworth's on her finger. The people from the parish felt duty-bound to satisfy themselves that you hadn't anything left of value and weren't trying to cheat the system: only then would they supply tokens that could be exchanged for food.

Only certain shops would accept those tokens. The butcher would only supply offal, the baker would supply stale bread, and if we were lucky we would have a few stale cakes. The greengrocer would give bruised vegetables and occasionally bruised fruit. We had to have whatever was given to us—we were in no position to choose. No money was ever given—only tokens.

I don't know how long my family were on parish relief. It was much too painful a subject for my mom to talk about, and I was too young to know or understand. I must have some unknown knowledge of it somewhere in my memory, however, because the anger of the injustice of it all is still with me.

My mom used to pay a penny a week insurance for all of us. That was because of the high death rate of babies at that awful time. However, there were some people who couldn't afford that small amount, and if their babies died they would put the babies in a cardboard box; then, somehow, they had to raise or borrow half a crown to give to a gravedigger: he would take the box and put it in a grave he was digging at the time—to be shared with its new occupant.

My dad was fifty when I was born. I can only remember him being old and ill. The majority of the time he was out of work, being ill with bronchitis. Long before I started school he would sit with me and teach me arithmetic. He also taught me how to play dominoes: fives and threes constituted my first lessons. I could reckon up money long before I started school. I remember mom and dad spent a lot of time playing crib. I would keep the score for them. Moving the spent matchsticks up and down the board was easy, though I couldn't understand the rules of the game. They would say: "Fifteen four, fifteen five and one for his knob!" I hadn't a clue what that meant and still don't to this day.

I must have been only about two or three, but I vaguely remember great crowds gathering just outside of our house and my dad holding me high on his shoulders when the circus came to town, and I watched elephants parading along the High Bullen Wednesbury.

My elder brother Eric made up a bike from bits and pieces he had managed to collect from various places, and on his birthday the bike was finally launched—though not for long, for it fell to bits when he tried to ride it. He received a very nasty cut on his head. Mom had made him a birthday cake and had put a fancy wrapper round the cake. She bandaged Eric's head, then put the wrapper from the cake around the bandage and he went to bed feeling very sorry for himself! However, some of the actors from the theatre across the road from the houses heard about the accident and came over to our house on stilts, giving my brother the fright of his life when they knocked on the bedroom window and wished him happy birthday. My dad, unimpressed, put a hammer to what was left of the bike.

2

The great day mom had long been waiting for finally arrived. She was informed that we had been allocated a brand new four-bed-roomed council house.

How happy she was! She went around in a dream. All the furniture was scrubbed and polished, to make sure it would be right for the new house. I believe the rent was eight shillings a week—a large amount and double the rent of the old house. My mom, though, was a great optimist and a very determined lady. She had made up her mind that her children were going to have a better home and we were going to have that house, come what may. Although mom was a kind and gentle woman where the health and happiness of her children were concerned, she could be a tigress. We never went hungry, though I'm quite sure that she did.

The poor working-class people were down and the system intended that they should stay down. They were meant to know their place and their place was right at the bottom of the pile.

There was no financial help at all in those days and, owing to my dad being out of work for such a long time, I don't believe he had much money in the way of sick pay. It was a constant struggle to pay that rent, but I know it was always paid on time.

Now that we had a four-bedroomed house, the sleeping arrangements were much easier.

Mom and dad finally had a proper bedroom for themselves. Grandma had a large bedroom while the two boys shared one room and us three girls shared the other. However, we still had to sleep three to the one bed, for we couldn't afford any luxuries like new beds. We didn't have pillows, but had one large bolster that the three of us could use. For some unknown reason our bed was pushed up against the wall and I was the one who slept closest to the wall. Some mornings when I woke up, my nose would be squashed into the wall—a circumstance that didn't do my face any good at all. (As far as I can remember, it didn't harm the wall anyway!) We slept on an old iron bedstead with knobs at the top and bottom. The knobs unscrewed which made a great secret hiding place for my pennies and half pennies.

Mom went around that house in a dream! She loved every part of it, but her favourite place was the bathroom with its big white clean bath and lovely hot water straight out of the tap—a luxury she never had before. She would get up at six o' clock each morning and soak in hot water. When we had a bath we all knew we had to leave the bath spotlessly clean, without any tidemarks or we would have been in real trouble. To my mom it was more like a shrine than a bath.

Some of our neighbours weren't as particular as my mom and found many more uses than bathing for *their* baths. One family kept the coal in their bath; another family of boys used theirs as a toilet, although the coalhouse and the toilet were under cover just outside of the back door. One old lady found an ingenious way of using the bath and making money at the same time: she made ginger beer and lemonade in the bath which she then sold for a penny a bottleful. We had to take our own bottle that she would fill by putting the bottle and her hand into the bath, sometimes sticking her arm in right up to her elbow and scooping up the concoction. I dread to think just what the health authorities would make of that method today, but I had many a pennyworth of that brew and it didn't do me any harm for I'm still here to tell the tale!

We were always sent to school clean, warm and tidy, although we didn't have many changes of clothing. Mom would wash our clothes after we had gone to bed, then put them on the clotheshorse by the fire to dry overnight. In the morning she would patch or darn the clothes, then iron and air them even before we were awake. Often there would be more darns and patches than the original material; but we never felt strange because everyone else was in the same boat. The only difference was that our clothes were put on clean each day, whereas some of the children wore the same dirty clothes all week. Some of the boys would continually wipe their noses on their sleeves so their jerseys looked and smelled quite disgusting by the end of the week. (Many years later I met two very well dressed brothers who had always done that and I asked them if they still wiped their noses on their sleeves; they got their own back on my birthday by going on to the stage of the pub which we kept and singing "She's thirty-three today!" because I wouldn't tell the customers my age—but that's another story.)

We always had a piece of old blanket or towel for a handkerchief. Many of the children would go to school unwashed, tired and hungry, and many had jobs to do before going to school. Some had to collect wood and chop the wood into small pieces, then go round the houses selling the wood for a penny a bundle; if they collected enough money they would go to the corner shop for a packet of margarine and a loaf of bread. If, however, they didn't collect enough money, they would have to go to school without any breakfast. Often, when they were warm from the classroom fire, they would fall asleep at their desks, and the teachers would leave them like that, sometimes for hours at a time. Perhaps they got more peace and quiet at school, maybe even more comfort, though they certainly didn't learn a lot!

The Black Country was certainly not known for the elite in the nineteen thirties. We wore lots of underclothes to keep us warm, for there wasn't any central heating in those days. It used to take ages to get dressed and undressed. First came the long vest with short sleeves, then a liberty bodice with buttons down the front. (Why it was called a liberty bodice I will never know, for it didn't allow much liberty of movement.) Next came the most tortuous garments of all—the 'combinations.' How I hated to wear those horrid things! They were an all-in-one garment with rubber buttons down the front, and then carrying on up to the backside. All the buttons at the lower front and behind had to be undone to go to the toilet! Next to the combinations came the long flannelette knickers that went all the way down to the knees;

then the long black stockings held up with garters. The top of the stockings would be pushed into the legs of the knickers. Then came at least two underskirts, then a top skirt and jumper, and finally a cardigan. Most of the garments would be several sizes too big for us, having been discarded from better-off cousins. But at least we were never cold. When we had holes in our socks or stockings, mom would darn, and often cut up two or more pairs of socks, stitching the best parts together to make one good pair. I still remember how the stitches rubbed into the instep. Often one pair of socks would be two or more different colours and sizes.

I used to lie in bed listening to mom mending our shoes. She used to do all those kind of jobs, for my dad couldn't knock a nail in straight. Mom, however, could and did everything to try to make life easier for us all. She really despaired when she came to mend my shoes, for I walked on the side of the heels and that made the shoes so much harder to repair. She would put thick cardboard inside the shoes to try to stop the nails sticking into my feet. After a while, though, the nails worked through and caused my feet to bleed. But I much preferred my feet to bleed than having to wear my grandma's boots.

How I hated those boots! They buttoned up to the knees and were several sizes too big. I sobbed and cried, and my mom sobbed and cried with me, but when I had no other shoes I still had to wear them. The other children laughed at me, saying I was wearing 'Cowboy Boots.'

My paternal grandma wasn't born into the working class. She came from a very well off Quaker family. She used to tell us stories of when she and her sister rode to fox hunting. They were privately educated. At one time my grandparents owned several shops and a factory, but they went bankrupt. I remember when grandma's still rich sister came to visit us from London. All the while she was at our home I would be guessing how much money she would give us when she left. Often it would be five shillings, which was a fortune to me, being more than a whole year's pocket money. I was quite mercenary and wished she would come to our house more often. I don't believe she ever offered any financial help to the family, although it was obvious she was in a position to do so.

It appears I was my grandma's favourite. I can still remember her very well. She was tall and very straight-backed, always spotlessly clean. Her dresses were beautifully cut and adorned with beads and sequins. She wore her dresses long, almost to her ankles, and every day she wore a different cravat round her neck. Her hair was beautifully white. She had a very grand 'Air' and was known by everyone as the 'Duchess.' It was quite plain to see by her bearing that she had had good breeding, money and education. She was a real character. It was very hard for her to adapt to a lower standard of living, all of her money having gone a long, long time before I came on the scene. My grandma was born around 1860.

My dad was 38 when he married mom, and she was only 25. Grandma must have thought he would never marry! She hung on to him and didn't like the idea of letting him go. In those days unmarried people always handed over their wage packets to their mother: it made no difference whether they were Fourteen or Forty! That was the general rule at that period. So it must have been a real shock to grandma when dad did finally get married. She lived with them and tried to insist on dad still handing over his wage packet to her. My mom was having none of that, of course. Grandma also tried to insist on having the first cut of meat!

It wouldn't surprise me that there was quite a lot of friction between them, mainly over us children. Although my mom was a quiet, gentle and thoughtful person, she certainly wouldn't be browbeaten by any-one—though I'm quite sure grandma gave her a hard time.

I would never fight with the other children in the street and it wasn't long before I was being bullied. When they all realised I was fair game they made my life a complete misery. I would go out to play and some of the children would be waiting for me and then set upon me. I would run back indoors, expecting to get the love and comfort of my mom's arms; but grandma must have got really fed up with my crying, for one day I didn't get the sympathy I was expecting. She grabbed me, turned me around to the door, and pushed me back outside with the words: "If thee cannot fight back, then shake them till their teeth rattle; and if thee ever come in crying again, I will hit thee as well!"

I was much more scared of grandma than I was of any of the children, so I went out and fought back and never had any more trouble. Where I was concerned, grandma's bark was worse than her bite. Nevertheless, I didn't intend to take any chances.

All week grandma had promised me she would take me to the fair on the Saturday afternoon. I counted each day off, and very early Saturday morning I awoke, grabbed my one and only possession, a knitted doll that I loved very much. By now, though, it was about four times its original size. I jumped out of bed with my doll in my arms, ran into grandma's room to remind her it was Saturday, and more important that it was 'Pocket Money' day and the great day for my long awaited treat. She was lying in her bed with her eyes wide open. I climbed onto her bed to speak to her, but she didn't answer me. I couldn't understand just why my grandma was ignoring me. I shook her arm and, still getting no response, I became frightened. I begged her to get dressed, to talk to me, to do *anything*, but not just ignore me. Although I was only six I realised that something was very wrong.

I rushed into my parents' room, telling them that grandma wouldn't speak to me. They both jumped out of bed and ran into her room.

Grandma was dead. She would never speak to me again.

She now lay in bed with a sheet over her face. Two pennies were placed on her eyes. Those two pennies really worried me, but I couldn't bring myself to ask anyone just why the pennies were on grandma's eyes. Would the pennies be buried with her? I really hoped not, for I really knew my mom couldn't afford the loss of even those pennies. I seemed to have a fixation about those pennies and worried more and more about the loss of them. Although I loved my grandma very much I knew even then the value of money—for it dawned on me that now she was dead I would be half a penny a week worse off!

Neighbours and family came to pay their respects to grandma. My dad told me to kiss her face. He told me not to be afraid. She had never hurt me when she was alive and certainly wouldn't hurt me now she was dead, he said.

I wasn't afraid, although her face was cold and still. It didn't seem like my grandma at all!

After a couple of days some men came and put her in a coffin that was left open on top of the bed. I would stand by the door and look in, but I wouldn't go too far into the room because I didn't like the smell. After a couple of more days the coffin was sealed. The smell, though, seemed to linger around the house for months.

The neighbours had a house-to-house collection for a wreath for grandma. They all had their upstairs and downstairs curtains closed, from the day she died until after the funeral, as a mark of respect for her and our family. People came from all over the estate to stand outside our house to see the flowers and watch the funeral procession go by. After the funeral was all over, a meal the neighbours had helped to prepare was provided for the mourners.

3

One day my eleven-year-old brother came home from school crying. The Headmistress had given him the cane because he couldn't do his long division sums.

When we moved house we all had to move to different schools and my brother tried to explain to the Headmistress that he hadn't been taught those sums at his other school. She didn't believe him and, instead of explaining the sums to him, she did the usual and easiest thing teachers did at that time—she caned him. He was terribly upset because he had got the cane through no fault of his own. And no matter how hard he tried, he couldn't master those sums. I was just six at the time but I remember sitting with him at the wooden table and explaining just how to do those long division sums. We managed to work the sums through. Ever since I can remember figures have always held a great magic to me. No one had ever taught me how to do those sums but somehow I knew by instinct what I was doing was right.

I found it very hard to learn to read and write, however. The teachers weren't known for their patience. It certainly wasn't their fault, for each class had at least forty children. The majority of them didn't want to learn anything at all. I wanted to learn, but it was very hard for me to understand. My brother, though, decided to return the favour I had done for him with the sums and so he sat with me at the same kitchen table. He spent many hours going through the alphabet and trying to teach me to read simple words. He told me I must keep on trying to master the words, and once I had, the whole wide world would open up for me.

How very right he was! I eventually became a bookworm.

Now, through my knowledge of reading, I could, and did, escape into my dream world. I swam the channel, flew over the Atlantic single-handed (of course), travelled down the Nile, saw the Pyramids, flew over the Rockies and I lived on Treasure Island. I was always the Head Prefect at some very posh boarding school that only catered for children of the very rich. I was always Jo in my favourite story *Little Women*. A handsome prince would enter my life, fall madly in love with me, then carry me off on his white charger; we always rode off into the sunset and, of course, we managed to live happily ever after.

Reality, though, was far from my dreams, for I was a big, plump child! I always had to have my hair cut very short. At the sides it was cut level with the top of my ears, but the awful part about it was the back that was sheared like a boy's hair. I really hated that and would cry when it was time to have it cut. I still had to submit to the ordeal, nevertheless, for short hair meant clean hair—and my mom had a great thing about cleanliness.

One of our neighbours had a shed in his back garden which, after his day's work, he used for his sideline—hair cutting. Often there would be a long queue waiting in his back garden even before he had arrived home from work. I would be in the queue, still crying, even when it was my turn to sit in the chair. (I seem to have spent a great deal of my childhood crying!) He would charge two pence for children and three pence for adults.

I wore very thick glasses and had a cast in my left eye of which I was very conscious, and which I couldn't help. All the children called me 'Cock eyes or four eyes.' I was told I had an idle eye! Looking back makes me realise I must have been a very scared, timid and insecure child. I had to go to the eye hospital quite regularly. Most of the time that didn't bother me at all. It meant time off school. It also meant that for a few hours I had my mom all to myself—which was great because at home her time had to be shared equally between us all. She would give me two pence and I would run ahead to the corner shop to get two pennyworths of broken biscuits. The bag would be full to overflowing. We had to travel on two different buses, and while we were on those buses we would both be munching through the bag of biscuits. I always searched through the bag to reach the best bits—the little bits of chocolate biscuits that always seemed to be at the very bottom of the bag. I always made very sure that all those biscuits were eaten long before we arrived home. I didn't intend to share them with my brothers and sisters, for that was my special treat, my secret that was shared only with my mom.

One day, when getting the biscuits, I spent my penny pocket money on a 'Lucky bag' that contained a few sweets and something else. I opened it very quickly to find the most beautiful ring I had ever seen in my life—and it was mine, mine alone! I tried it on my finger which, of course, it fitted perfectly. I felt like a queen! I just knew that I would always wear it, and that it was mine for life.

I excitedly showed my treasure to mom, who suitably admired it. I was so happy with my ring that I forgot for a while that I had to go into the 'Dreaded dark room'—the one room which held so much terror for me. Mom always tried to enter that room with me. She tried to take away my fears by going into the room with me. But she was always turned away at the door. I never could understand why she wasn't allowed into the room. I would hang on tight to mom, hoping she could slip into the room without anyone noticing, but it wasn't to be. A nurse would pull me away from mom and drag me screaming into the pitch-dark room that I was so very much afraid of.

In those days no one ever questioned people in authority. My mom had told me the doctors were trying to make my eyes better and I trusted my mom. She was the only person I did trust, but that room held so much terror for me.

When my eyes got accustomed to the dark I saw a man with no hair at all. His head was shiny and looked like an egg. By now I was *really* petrified. I stood as near to the door as possible, hoping that at the very first chance I could run out of that horrible room, straight back into the safety of my mom's comforting and loving arms. But the man shouted at me, saying he hadn't got all day to waste on me. The nurse pushed and shoved me into a chair and the man came closer and closer, staring into my eyes that were full of tears. He made me look into a machine that appeared to have two tunnels, one for each eye. In the one tunnel there was a picture of a lion, in the other a cage. I had to turn two handles and the idea was for me to manoeuvre the lion into the cage. But I couldn't do it however hard I tried! He then removed the slides with the lion and cage, replacing them with slides of a soldier and a sentry box. Again I had to try to put the soldier with his red uniform and gun into the sentry box! By now I was in a terrible state and was so frightened I couldn't do anything right. I was shaking and crying and the man became very impatient with me.

Then, suddenly, he noticed my treasured ring! He snatched up my hand and, holding my wrist with one hand, pulled off my beautiful ring with his other hand. He said I shouldn't wear such rubbish, that it would stick into my finger and cause blood poisoning. He then threw my 'Prize Possession' into the waste-paper basket! At the great age of six I hadn't any knowledge of blood poisoning, but I did know a great deal about poverty, ridicule and unhappiness.

Looking back, now, it seems obvious the Doctor (although I hesitate to call him Doctor) was having a bad day—and I'm sure my fears didn't help any. But it was surely plain for anyone to see that I was heartbroken at losing my ring! Perhaps at the end of the day he went home and felt some remorse; perhaps—just perhaps—he might even have lost some sleep.

I know that I did

The callousness, the roughness and the lack of compassion and understanding hurt me still—so much, in fact, that apart from my engagement and wedding rings, I have never in my life worn any other rings.

4

The fireplace was the focal point of the living room. I always sat as near to the fire as possible, and being a great dreamer and having a vivid imagination I could see the coal, flames and ashes turn into faces, mountains, rivers and all sorts of wonderful things.

With progress, the coal fire has now gone. In its place we have radiators. A person would have to have a very vivid imagination to see pictures in a radiator. After our bath we would sit close by the fire while mom combed and dried our hair. Our clothes would be warming on the hob. We dressed and undressed, getting closer and closer to the fire. All the family gathered round and we would talk and talk. Sometimes we played guessing games, dominoes or cards. We always played for money. I would have my little pile of half pennies. I was quite lucky at cards and often would beat my brothers and finally end up with their money, which I never felt the tiniest bit bothered about taking! Often we would turn out the lights, and with just the glow from the fire we would sit around the fireplace telling stories, jokes or repeating the gossip of the day. Sometimes we had a singsong. *Just a song of Twilight* was the family favourite.

The grate was old fashioned, and black-leaded every morning by mom until we could see our faces in it. There was an oven at the side that cooked very, very slowly. Sometimes the food was put into the oven very early in the morning, taking all day to cook, ready for the evening meal. The aroma hit our nostrils the very moment we came from school and opened the back door. Mom had a large stew-pot, and everything seemed to go into that pot.

Often we would get out the long toasting fork, taking it in turns to toast ourselves and the bread, which was then spread with pork dripping. The dog was always banished from the hearth, but somehow he always managed to creep back there when he thought no one was looking. There was a large peg rug on the hearth. We had all helped to cut the very old coat material into strips, and mom 'podged' the small pieces of material onto the backs of sugar bags. Those rugs lasted for years, but were very hard to make: often our fingers blistered and bled with the continuing cutting of the material.

The coal fire was a time-consuming job. Wood had to be chopped, ashes raked, with the sorting out of the bits that could be re-used. Coal was broken into small pieces and then carried from the coalhouse. The coal fire really was hard work and belongs to that bygone age when mothers didn't go out to work and waited for their children to come from school, greeting them with a hug, a warm smile, a cup of tea and an invitation to sit by the fire to get warm.

Our living room was very crowded with seven of us. I always had my nose in a book, and being the only bookworm in the family I was constantly being teased by my brothers and sisters. It became impossible to read and make my great escape into my world of dreams with all the rough and tumble of family life. So I soon found myself an escape route. I would get a cushion and take it into the bathroom, which was the only room in the house with a lock; the back boiler of the fire was also located there, which meant that apart from the living room it was the only room in the house that was really warm enough to linger in. (The bedrooms were freezing cold; furthermore, I had to share my bedroom with my two sisters!) And so, I would reach two blankets out of the airing cupboard, place one long-ways in the bath, and place my cushion at the other end from the taps. I would then take off my shoes and climb into the bath, wrapping the other blanket around me.

I managed to stay there for hours at a time in warmth and reasonable comfort, but best of all in perfect peace and quiet, until someone realised I was missing and would come banging on the bathroom door, shouting for me to go and do some work!

Now that I found a way to embark on my adventures I was the greatest escapologist since Houdini, living and breathing my wonderful world of books. The bathroom was also my hiding place when 'The Aunts,' my mom's elder sisters, came, for they would make a big fuss of my younger sister Margaret who was small, dainty and beautiful, whereas I was big, plump and wore horrible thick glasses! I suffered from a massive inferiority complex that sat down hard on both my shoulders. The Aunts complimented my sister, making a great fuss of her, and then, only as an afterthought would turn to me, saying, "Haven't you grown!" I hated that and would be consumed with jealousy. My refuge saved me if I had the chance to escape before their arrival. It also saved my sister from having a thumping from me, for I always managed to take out my frustration and anger out on her—which wasn't really fair since none of it was her fault.

There were five classrooms at school, a dreary place though it wasn't an old school. The windows were always kept closed and the walls were painted dark green and grey—horrible dismal colours. There were no pictures or paintings to brighten the place up, no flowers, no visible signs at all of friendliness or happiness. We all sat on double hard benches. The desks had double tops so we had to open two desks in one go. There were ten children in a row and four rows to a class. We all sat facing the teacher's desk, which was raised, and always in the right-hand side of the room. Against the middle of the room was a fireplace with a roaring fire. When the fire went low the teacher sent a child to find the caretaker, who would come and re-stoke it.

I remember the awful smell of unwashed children. We were as poor as any of the others, but my mom always waged a one-woman war against dirt. Each morning she would get out the carbolic soap and really scrub at the back of my neck, so much that I made a vow to myself that when I grew up I would never wash my neck again!

Four of the teachers made no impression on me at all. But one teacher made up for all the others! She was great, but her nose really fascinated me, for it was large, *really* large, and it curled up at the end. I would imagine hanging my coat on the end of her nose and it staying there all day. This one teacher loved arithmetic and she must have realised I felt the same way, for she certainly got through to me—so much so that by the time I was seven I had to go into her class of ten and eleven year olds. That was great at first, but it meant I had the same lessons for at least four years—and never had the opportunity to progress further.

The Black Country in the 1930's was peopled mainly with working-class poor people, and the general idea at that time was that any child coming from a poor working-class family couldn't be clever; in fact, a clever child was ridiculed mainly because the teachers didn't know how to handle the situation. I never put up my hand to answer a question and I often pretended I didn't know the answers to the questions asked me, mainly because I hated having attention drawn to me. I had the great misfortune of being a clever child at the wrong time. There was a great deal of talent wasted because of the class system of that time and the ignorance of the so-called teachers. I can only remember the one story that was read to us—*The Wind in the Willows*. I have a copy still. I also have a copy of a book given to us at school by the mayor and chairman of the education committee to commemorate the coronation of the king and queen in May 1937. It's the most 'twee' book I have ever read, and occasionally I will glance through it even now, just to remind myself—if I ever need reminding!—just how things were then. The book starts by saying, "Most of us expect a king's home to be a palace. But our king, when he was little, lived in a cottage." To imply that the king was brought up in a cottage and was on a par with families who were near to the breadline I find truly amazing and deeply offensive. Mom had knitted red, white and blue berets for Margaret and me for the coronation.

I hated that school! It was an unhappy time and place for me. I was a dreamer and it certainly wasn't the time or place for dreamers. The Headmistress was a screwed-up, frustrated sex-starved old maid who got her kicks by terrifying defenceless children. For some unknown reason I always seemed to be her prime target. Throughout the day I would listen for the sound of her heavy footsteps thumping down the corridor, watch out for the handle of the door slowly, very slowly turning, and even before she entered the room I was already shaking and trembling with fear. I knew everyone in the class knew she would make straight for me! She would make me stand up and then she would ask, "What are nine times five?!" She knew very well that I knew the answer; she also knew that I couldn't pronounce the letter *F*. However hard I tried I just couldn't say "Forty Five." She would make me try to say it over and over again! Each time I got worse and became more flustered.

The teacher would be embarrassed. I would squirm, wishing the floor would open and swallow me up. The children laughed at my utter misery, well knowing that while I was having the 'Treatment' *they* were all right. It was only when I broke down in a flood of tears that she was fully satisfied.

Her life must have been so completely barren and empty to get such great satisfaction out of making my life a misery.

Now I only feel a great pity for her wasted life, and for all the happiness that clearly had passed her by. I really feared and hated her! Our lives were hard enough without any help from her. She should never have been allowed within a mile of any child.

Once, during playtime, I was sitting on the hall steps, reading as per usual, when a hand grabbed my shoulder. Rudely awakening from my dreams, I looked up to see the one person who sent cold shivers down my spine. She pulled me to my feet and ordered me to wait outside her room. I did know that it was against the rules to play on those hall steps, but I didn't really think that the same rules applied to just sitting—and reading—on them.

I waited a long time, trembling outside her door, until she finally emerged. Without saying one word, she pointed her finger and beckoned me into her room; then, reaching for a long thin cane she kept hanging on a peg above her desk, she ordered me to hold out my hands. The cane came down first on one hand and then the other.

She wanted me to cry. We both knew that, but I prayed harder than ever in my life—*please, please* don't let me cry! I bit hard into the inside of my mouth until it bled. The smile on her face began to disappear when she realised this was one time she wasn't going to get the better of me. The physical hurt I could take, but the mental torture she gave me left scars that lasted a long, long time.

One of the lady teachers left and for the first time ever the school had a man teacher.

Named Mr Phillips, he would throw chalk, rulers, or anything that came to hand at the pupils. One day he noticed a boy sitting in front of me was talking. He removed his shoe and threw it at the boy. The boy noticed the shoe flying through the air and quickly ducked out of harm's way. I wasn't so quick. The shoe hit me on the forehead. The teacher didn't bother to apologise: in fact, I had to take the shoe back to him, which was adding insult to injury.

On the way to school was a large manor house that belonged to the local industrialist. It had large grounds, and there was an orchard and a tennis court. I used to peep through a tiny hole in the fence at the family playing tennis. At the side of the house there was a long passageway that had a window looking into the back of the house. The children would dare each other to run the length of the passage and then look into the window without being caught.

Some children said there was a large brown bear tied up in the room; others said there was a ghost. When it was my turn to run the passageway I did the world's first four-minute mile! Quickly looking into the window as I ran, I didn't see either the brown bear or the ghost.

The lady of the manor was the second wife who had been hired as a governess for the children. When the mother died she married the father. She had a great opinion of herself, for she was a school governor and often made visits to the school. She arranged for the apples and pears that were windfalls to be delivered to the school. She would then grace us with her presence at assembly. The headmistress would make a gushing speech, thanking her on the children's behalf for her kindness. We then had to form two lines in long queues and she would give each of us either a worm-eaten apple or pear! With the headmistress breathing down our necks we each had to give our thanks again.

When the industrialist lay dying, sawdust was put down on the road for as far as the eye could see, just to deaden the noise of the traffic. When he died both sides of the street were lined with people. Most of the large industrial factories were closed for the day.

We hadn't any toys so we made up our own games. Our favourite was playing shops. We used broken platter as money. Large pieces became two shillings and half crowns; small pieces were pennies, three-penny bits, sixpences and shillings. Bricks, dirt, grass and weeds were pretend food. A piece of wood balanced on a stone became our scales. Margaret and I used to argue about whose turn it was to be shop-keeper. Other games we played were 'tip cat,' which was a small piece of wood shaped to a point at both ends and a stick, the idea being to get the stick and hit the small piece of wood into the air, then hit it again before it could reach the ground: the winner was the one who could hit the wood the most times before it fell down to the ground.

We played cricket and used lampposts as stumps. Lampposts would also serve as goal posts for football, jumpers and coats being placed around the gutters for corners. We had to wait, though, until the children who possessed a ball came out to play—and then they would be the bosses! They would decide who could play and who couldn't, and would pick the best players for their team.

After we'd been playing for perhaps an hour their mothers would call them in for their tea, and they would take the ball with them—which meant we had to hang around until they decided to come out again! If they didn't, then we were back to square one. If the ball went into the gardens we always got a telling off, but we were really scared if the ball went into the garden of one old lady, for she was *really* a dragon! All the kids were terrified of her. She shouted at us all and always kept the ball, saying she was going to put it on the fire. We were all convinced she was collecting the balls for her grandchildren.

I think I was about eight when the school started doing dinners, and any child who hadn't a dad, or who had a dad not at work, was allowed free dinners. My dad had been ill a long time so I qualified for the dinners. We were given tokens to exchange for the meal. I entered the canteen and joined the long queue, moving one step, then waiting. I really was hungry, for the aroma of the food had by then reached my nostrils and I was really looking forward to my meal. With the token in my hand I finally reached the counter. On trying to hand it over to the assistant I was told to wait across the room until the children who had paid were served; then, and only then, after the paying children were catered for, we, the free dinner children, could be served with whatever was left over. Although I loved my food and really wanted that lunch, I walked hungrily out of that canteen. One thing that couldn't ever be taken away from me was my pride—something my mom had deeply installed in me. I didn't believe I would ever be so hungry as to eat all that 'Humble Pie.'

The short time my dad was well enough to work I would take his lunch to his workplace. It was quite a rush for me. I had to run the mile from school and mom would meet me at the gate with the lunch in a basin. A saucer sat on top to keep it warm, a tea towel wrapped around it with the ends tied into a loop to slip my fingers through. I then had to walk very quick, not run, lest the gravy be spilt. I had to get to the factory gate just before the bulls went. (The bulls were the sirens which each factory had.) The bulls seemed to control everyone's lives, whether we were at work or not; they would sound to tell people when to go to work, when to stop work, when to eat, when to do everything. (Well, nearly everything!) The continuous noise went on day and night, each factory bulls having their own particular tone. We always knew the time of day without looking at any clocks. (No one could ever afford to buy watches.)

Just as I reached the factory gate the men began to stream out. Dad would take his lunch from me and try to find a quiet corner to eat his lunch in peace. I then had to run all the way back home, gulp down my own lunch, and run back to school, all the time hoping I wouldn't be late, for if I were I'd be in serious trouble.

We used to think up all sorts of ways to make money because mom couldn't afford to give us much pocket money. One thing I found to be quite lucrative was taking the neighbours' bets to the 'Bookie.' In those days there were no betting shops, but there was always a back street bookie. In fact, there was a back street everything, if you knew where to look, and I always kept my nose to the ground. Anyway, the neighbours gave me a penny a week, plus extra if they won and felt in a generous mood. The bookie also gave me two pence. I was doing all right, or rather, I would have been if I hadn't acquired the gambling habit myself at a very early age. I would study the racing page of the morning paper and then pick out the horses I fancied. I would then place a bet of either a penny or two pence each way, depending on how my finances were at the time. We all had nicknames in our family, mine being 'Pud' for obvious reasons. I would put my *Nom de plume* on the slip so that the bookie would know whose bet it was. I then eagerly listened to the races on the wireless, getting quite excited and urging my horses on to win. If I did have any winners or place wins I would add up the total without the aid of a calculator (the only calculator I used was the one in my head which was always spot on!). In a flash I then ran to the bookie, telling her how much I had won and saying I had come to claim my winnings. She would exclaim, "You haven't won *that* much! Count it up again!" I would become quite angry and would go all through the bet with her. She knew I could reckon the odds on the horses just as quickly and as accurately as she could. I didn't realise at that time, of course, that she was only teasing me, for I had a terrible temper and was very, very serious where money was concerned—especially when it was *my* money!

When I was about eight I worked for the bookie on Saturday afternoons by sitting in the gutter outside of her house, looking all innocent, as if butter wouldn't melt in my mouth. But I was doing a job of work. I was waiting to see if a policeman was about to appear. The bookie's house was quite a way up the street, and if I saw him turn round the corner into the street I had plenty time to jump up and run into the house to warn her of his approach. The police knew she was an illegal bookie, I've no doubt. I believe it was just routine checks they made, more like a game between them, for she never got caught. She had two bags, one for the money and the other for the betting slips. Someone was always there to run down the garden with the bags, go through a hole in the fence (made deliberately, of course), run through another garden and into the back street. The policeman would have a quick search of the house, then jump onto his bike and go. I always watched until he turned the corner, and then ran into the back street to give the 'all clear.' I received an extra three-penny bit for that.

My older sister saved up all her money until she had five shillings. Then she bought an old bike. All the children queued up to have a ride and she charged everyone, including me, a half penny to go down our street, and a penny to go farther into the next street. I paid my penny, then cycled like mad to go into three streets for my penny's worth—without her knowing. (Otherwise it would have cost me an extra half penny.) There were no reductions for extra rides, or for being a sibling. Needless to say she soon recovered her initial stake. She also made up plays and concerts that only had the one player—'Herself'—in which she wore grandma's long beaded dresses, the charge this time being a penny. It was a charge I still had to pay, although the 'Shows' were performed in our bedroom! I seem to recall that quite a lot of children attended those shows.

We also used to sell or exchange comics. It depended on whether we had any money at that particular time. One boy came to buy, but he always insisted on going through each page. He sat on our kitchen floor and very carefully read the comics from the beginning to the end.

He would say, "I've already read those comics—I don't think I'll bother buying any today." He never even gave us the chance to look at *his* comics.

Near neighbours of ours would go to the pub on Saturday nights and, although their daughter was only a couple of years younger than me, I would baby-mind her and her young brother. We played out until it got dark, then we would go into their house. There were two horsehair settees: the girl went to sleep on the one and the lad slept on the other while I had to sit on a hard uncomfortable kitchen chair and rest my head on the table. About ten minutes before closing time Margaret would knock on the door and I would let her in; and when the parents came home they would give us a shilling each, which was then a large amount of money for us. Their children had slept most of the time so they didn't know just how long Margaret had been in the house.

There was one little girl I really loved. Her mom used to put her in her pram, give me a penny and I would push the pram up and down the street for hours at a time. One day when the mother was carrying the baby to the corner shop, I crept up behind her and shouted, 'Boo!' The baby very nearly jumped out of her mom's arms and the mother was furious with me. She gave me a right telling off and said I could have caused the baby to have a fit! I was really scared, worrying about the harm I could have unintentionally done to the baby. I had a few sleepless nights worrying myself sick about that baby, and each day I went around her house straight from school to see if she was all right. I was very relieved to find she was fine. I thought there *had* to be a better way to earn some pennies without all that worry, so I abandoned the baby-minding business.

5

Once a year we had our photos taken at school. We would always take them home to show mom but she hardly had enough money to feed us all, so photos were a luxury we couldn't afford. I still remember my great humiliation when I had to return the photos to school the next morning and say that my mom hadn't the money for them. Perhaps in my case it was just as well I had to return them, for I often wore a big black patch covering my good eye; sometimes I had plaster strips put on my glasses which probably did more harm than good because I always tried to see between the strips. So with my short boyish hair, either the patch on my eye or the strips on my glasses, I couldn't have been a pretty sight.

There are no photos of us as children at all. For myself, I don't need photos to remind me of those terrible times. I really wish, though, that there were just one photo to show my grandchildren. Perhaps it would have given them a good laugh.

On my birthday mom always asked me if I wanted a birthday card or a three-penny bit—a silly question, really, since she knew me well enough to know that I realised the value of money. Of course, I always asked for the money—every time. Somehow, though, she managed to provide the card *and* the three-penny bit.

One of mom's younger sisters (not to be confused with the Aunts who were much older) sent me a present through the post for every one of my birthdays. She could easily have brought the present to our home, but she knew the great pleasure I received by having a parcel come to the door—a parcel addressed to me alone! I always ran every inch of the way home from school on my special day; then, I would take great pleasure examining the parcel and turning it this way and that, trying to guess what was inside while holding off the magic moment for as long as possible. Finally my family would get impatient with me, and when I couldn't contain my excitement one second longer, I would carefully undo the string which I would roll into a ball for re-use, then fold the brown paper again for the same reason. I had been very well schooled in economics by my mom's example. Then, at last, the marvellous moment—to see my present! Mine alone, not to be shared with anyone! Usually it was a book, or paints and a drawing book. Sometimes, though, it was cardboard cut-out dolls with different outfits. Once it was a little leather purse with K H—my initials—stamped into the leather, which I thought was great. (I loved that purse and used it for many years; in fact, it lasted long enough for my daughters to play with.)

Approaching Christmas, I would wait until mom had gone shopping; then I would drag the old sofa near to the cupboard where I knew my presents where hidden. Then, very carefully, I would place a chair on top of the sofa; then climb, wobbling about, stretching right to the back of the cupboard and with the tips of my fingers, I would just manage to pull the book forward. (It was always a book!) Then I would climb down, making a quick dive into my haven, the bathroom. I would have to read through the book rapidly before repeating the entire process with the sofa and chair—in reverse! Holding onto the cupboard with one hand, I would try to push the book back into the exact same place as before. Dad was ill in bed so I knew he wouldn't know just what I was doing. I never knew if my mom ever found out about my escapades. I expect she did, although she never let on.

My friend told me her grandma had just died and asked me if I wanted to see the body. I was an inquisitive child, and as I had already seen my own grandma's body I said I would. She lived in an old terraced cottage. I remember going down a passageway between two cottages, then going into the scullery where all the family were sitting. My friend asked her mom if we could go into the front room, which was only ever used for Births, Weddings and Funerals—which was the custom in those days. We then went into that room, and later how I wished I had never gone anywhere near it! The curtains were drawn and it was quite dark. When my eyes had got used to the darkness I could see there was an old horsehair sofa and on it was the grandma's body.

She was the biggest and fattest person I had ever seen in my life.

She was huge!

Going farther into the room, I noticed there were buckets and bowls under the sofa. Water was seeping out of the body into the horsehair sofa and then through to the buckets and bowls. I was petrified! I turned around sharpish and ran out of that place and didn't stop running until I reached the safety of my own home. For months afterwards I had terrible nightmares.

One lady in our street was known as "Aunt Harriet" by everyone. I believe she was a retired nurse. People had to pay five shillings to visit or call in the doctor. They couldn't afford to send for the doctor when they were ill, so the cry would be, "Fetch Aunt Harriet!" The whole of the estate called on her services, but we thought we should have first claim on her because she lived in our street. Once I was playing in the road and a neighbour opened her window and shouted to me: "Quick, wench! Fetch Aunt Harriet and tell her my waters have broken!"

I didn't understand a word she had said, but I knew better than not to repeat the message word for word. I ran to Aunt Harriet and she gathered up her bits and pieces, hitched up her skirt and rushed as fast as she could. She seemed very old to me, but when you're very young, everyone else is ancient. She was perhaps in her early sixties. Aunt Harriet was our guardian angel and she lovingly attended to everyone, gave advice, tended the sick, told mothers when the children really needed a doctor, and bandaged cut knees. She was always called to lay out the dead, too. I don't know who lay out "Aunt Harriet" when her time came, but I do know she was an end of an era.

Although we were poor we didn't appreciate this. Everyone in the street was in the same situation. It was a way of life. We didn't know of any other way. The really poor families were the people without love.

In our family we were rich in having a unique mother who spent her whole life working to try to make our lives that little bit easier. Our neighbours on the one side were always quarrelling. My sister and I used to get inside of the floor-to-ceiling cupboard, and then put a drinking glass to the wall so that we could hear the argument and listen to some really choice swearwords. We found we could hear better through the glass. After a while, though, the arguments got louder and much worse, and we no longer needed the glass! At that point, in fact, we didn't even have to go into the cupboard. It got so bad that finally we could hear everything whichever room we were in!

My brother called another neighbour Mrs. 'Such-a-thing' for she would call round and ask, "Have you got such a thing as a needle and black cotton?"—or at other times it would be, "Have you got such a thing as a few pages of writing paper and an envelope?" My brother sarcastically asked her if she wanted a pen as well, but his sarcasm was lost on her, for she always answered, "No thank you, I've got a pen!"

I remember other neighbours with a large family. The mother was a timid little woman who couldn't say Boo to a goose. The father was a brute of a man who terrified his family and most of the people in the street—so much so that several families went to the council and asked to be re-housed somewhere else. If any women were chatting by their gates when he walked past he would tell them to get indoors and get on with their housework! When the children saw him coming they ran away like scared rabbits; even the cats and dogs scurried out of his way, for he always used to swing a kick at them.

Once, sitting on the wall in my usual dream state, I failed to notice him walking towards me until it was too late. He had a horrid grin on his face as he grabbed me by my arm and pulled me from the wall. "Get back into the house, you cockeyed little bugger!" he shouted. I was terrified and began to sob. I ran into the house, still sobbing and shaking. My mom tried to find out why I was crying and in such a terrible state, but I couldn't speak; and then, through my sobbing I managed to blurt out just what he had said.

A great change came over my quiet, gentle and placid mom. She was furious! She jumped up and marched over to his house. I tagged along, still sobbing, but I didn't want to miss anything. She walked straight into the house without knocking—something she wouldn't normally do. He was sitting on one side of the fireplace, his wife on the other side, his children sitting around the table. Mom rushed passed the wife and the children and charged up to him. She grabbed him by the scruff of his neck and belted into him with both fists flying.

All the family looked on in complete astonishment! No one moved an inch to try to stop mom—neither his wife nor either of his children lifted a hand to help him. And he didn't retaliate in any way—he just sat there cowering, sinking farther and farther down into his chair. He seemed to be getting smaller and smaller. It was perfectly clear to everyone in that room what a pathetic, cowardly little man he really was!

I was very proud of my mom. She really let rip, calling him everything except a gentleman.

I had never heard my mom swear before, and certainly never realised she had such a vivid vocabulary! When she finally turned to leave the room the eldest daughter (who was the only one of the children not terrified of him) jumped up, rushed to mom and threw her arms around her neck. She kissed and hugged her, saying he had it coming for a long while! She told mom she had intended to go to the cinema and had changed her mind at the last minute—thankfully, because what she had just seen was better than any film!

The next morning the mother came round to our house and, timidly knocking on the door, asked if she could come in. She apologised for her husband's behaviour and hoped mom wouldn't hold it against her. She needn't have worried, for mom invited her in, made a cup of tea and made her feel at home. She was a scared, lonely woman who had never been more than five miles away from where she was born! She had never been on a train or even a bus. She was a pathetic little woman with long grey hair that she plaited and then tied round her ears.

All of the neighbours would take their troubles to mom. They knew their business was safe with her, that she would never repeat anything. She would sit them down by the fire and make a cup of tea. Most of their troubles were financial anyway, and there was no way she could help them there. She had a sympathetic ear, so they always went from our house feeling better than when they entered it.

Houses had to be cleaned every day, the reason being all the dirt and grime that got into the houses from all the nearby factories. The women had to change the curtains in the whole house once a week because of the factory dust. Women who didn't change their curtains each week would be talked about and regarded as idle.

6

One of the neighbours used to parcel her husband's best suit plus anything else she thought of value into an old pram. My elder sister and I would take the lot to the pawnshop for her. Come Friday, when it was her husband's payday, we had to fetch the lot back again. We certainly didn't mind going backwards and forwards, for we were paid a penny each way. It was quite a lucrative business for us. It beat baby minding any day. It also meant I could have a good nose at other people's business, and the pawnshop window was a delight to me. There would be rings, watches, necklaces, brooches, bracelets, suits, dresses and all sorts of wonderful things. Inside there were shelves packed from floor to ceiling with all manner of clothing. Most of it had been there for months. The shop had a lovely musty smell of mothballs. I really loved to go to that shop. It reeked of atmosphere that no other place ever had. I would dawdle as long as possible so that I could know whatever anyone else was bringing in or taking out.

The pawnbroker was an old man. He kept an eyeglass in his top pocket and when anyone brought in jewellery he would get out the glass, face the light from the window, stare at the jewellery and mutter. Finally he would turn to the customer and say, "Hum, hum…I can only let you have four shillings for this." The woman who was pawning the jewellery would then say, "But it's worth *much* more than that! I have to have six shillings to put back into my husband's pocket before he finds out I've taken it, or he'll murder me!" The pawnbroker was used to all the sob stories; nothing was new for he had heard them all before. The stories went in one ear and out the other. Finally he would make an offer of five shillings, which was what she wanted in the fist place. She would go away happy and he would be happy too, knowing he couldn't lose, for she would return at the weekend to redeem the

43

jewellery and he had his commission just for letting her have the money for a few days. (If for any reason she didn't redeem the jewellery, by law he had to keep it safe for six months; then he was free to sell it for any price he could get, so either way he was a winner.)

Just writing about that pawnshop brings the smell of mothballs to my nose! The whole place reeked of them, especially when the pawnbroker climbed up a ladder to remove suits from the top shelf, perhaps disturbing the mothballs that had been there for months. With one hand he would reach to the back of the shelf and with the other hold on to the ladder for dear life. That man certainly lived dangerously! There was a thick wire mesh at the counter between him and the customers. I often pressed my nose close to the wire mesh so I didn't miss anything. At the same time I would be making up stories, and thinking if only those articles on the shelves could speak they would tell more unbelievable tales than even I with my vivid imagination could ever think of.

On one of my birthdays mom must have had a few coppers to spare, and as a special treat she promised to take me to the pictures to see Gracie Fields. To go to the pictures was a very rare and special treat but, to see Gracie as well was fantastic! The two people I loved most in the world were my mom and Gracie. I loved to hear Gracie on the wireless, but to actually *see* her was something really wonderful. I sat as quiet as a little mouse throughout the film watching her every move and listening open-mouthed to her singing. I was bursting with love and happiness—so much so that I really thought Gracie loved me in the same way! Turning to mom I asked, "Does Gracie know I'm here?" Mom answered, "I'm sure she does!" I couldn't fathom out why, if Gracie knew I was there, she didn't come and speak to me.

Mom would wait until late on Saturday evening to do the shopping, going about eight o'clock when the stallholders were ready to call it a day. No one had fridges or freezers in those days, so the stallholders had to sell off cheap any perishable food. She could buy a large joint of pork, beef, or lamb for sixpence, bits of bacon, and sausages for two pence. Next came the bread stall for stale bread, and a huge bag of stale cakes for a penny. (Margaret and I used to argue and sometimes fight for the creamiest cakes.) Cracked eggs were four for a penny. Mom would mash two eggs with a knob of margarine to make it spread out more; those two eggs made enough sandwiches for the whole family! The vegetable stall was the one I liked best of all. I could stand there for ages, completely mesmerised watching the lady serving on that stall. Whenever anyone gave her a ten-shilling note, she put it down her right stocking; a pound note went down her left stocking. No one in our circumstances ever had fivers or ten-pound notes. She didn't seem bothered about lifting up her dress, or of anyone seeing her legs and the top of her stockings. Down, down the notes would go! Just standing there and watching the notes going farther down her legs, and the bulge of her stockings growing larger, was utter magic for me. When she wanted a ten-shilling note for change, she plunged her hand into the right stocking. She never, but *never* mixed up either the notes or legs! By late evening her stockings were just about ready to burst with the volume of those notes. I thought she must have had very strong suspenders. Selling vegetables looked like a very profitable business: perhaps, I thought, I should consider being a greengrocer when I grew up!

Other stalls were called 'the shambles.' Second-hand clothes were piled up high and we would buy several different coloured old coats for a few pence to cut up to make the peg rugs. The more colours there were, the better pattern for the rugs. People almost fought to get to the front of the stall for the best bargains.

At another stall a man would give a bit of ballyhoo for the goods he was selling and to get a crowd to gather round to listen to him. This one time I must have thought he was really good, for I started to laugh and clap at his spiel. He was so pleased with me that he called me to the front of the stall and gave me a penny! I thought I was on to some easy money there, so I tried again the next week, but without the same success. Indeed, I was never so lucky ever again.

Mom and I always walked to the market, about two miles away. We had to save the bus fare (one penny for mom and a half penny for me) for the return journey when we would be laden with the shopping. One terribly cold and snowy day mom went shopping by herself. She wouldn't let me go with her—she said it was too cold for me to go out. She wrapped herself up warm and put on some woollen gloves and away she went. She was away a long, long time—so much longer than usual that we all became terribly worried wondering where she could possibly be. All of us were looking through the window and going to the gate to see if she was coming up the street. Finally we saw her turning the corner of the street. We ran to meet her to see if she was all right and to help her into the house.

She was frozen to the skin and her tears had frozen down her face! Her hands were blue with cold. She was carrying empty shopping bags. She had put all of the money she had for the week's shopping (a ten shilling note) in the inside of her gloves, and somehow she had lost the money. She had retraced her steps over and over again, but the money had gone for good.

If I live to be a hundred I will never forget the utter despair of my mom's kind gentle face.

I don't recall just how we managed to get through that week, but whoever found that money couldn't possibly have been poorer than we were. My mom never in her life wore gloves again when she went shopping, however cold the weather was. We used to have to remove the shopping bags from her fingers which would be blue with cold and then massage the life back into them.

We used to buy all our food, clothes, shoes, household goods and oilcloth from the market. We were never silly enough to ask the price of the goods. That would have been fatal, for the goods would have gone up in price straight away! Instead, we stood by the stall (sometimes for hours) while the stallholder held each article up; he would start with a high price and work down. Even then we waited, hoping he would drop the price farther, but it was very hard to judge the right time to put our hands up for the goods. If we waited too long someone else may have got ahead of us and grabbed the article we had waited so long for. (It was everybody for themselves out there!) Then all our waiting would have been for nothing. Sometimes, if an article wasn't sold, the stallholder would get annoyed and throw the article into the crowd and some lucky person would get it for free!

When we needed oilcloth we had to get to the market very early, to try to get to the front of the crowd. We arrived there long before the arrival of the lorry that was piled high with the oilcloth. There would be three men in the lorry. One would give us all the ballyhoo and the other two would take the orders and the money. We had to stand there for ages, first on one foot and then the other. It was very tiring waiting all that time without knowing what the outcome of our waiting would be, and at the same time being pushed and shoved one way and another. We would then indicate to each other which roll of oilcloth we all liked without letting the men know we were interested in that particular roll; at the same time we hoped it was the right length and, much more important, the right price. We also had to hope that no one else would beat us to the sale. Finally, when we did get the deal settled, mom had to pay two shillings extra for delivery which would be the same day after the men had finished their sales.

Getting that oilcloth was a great achievement. Mom had saved up for a long time to get those few shillings together, and we simply couldn't afford to make any mistakes. The really hard part came when the oilcloth was delivered—the fitting and laying, especially if it was for the stairs. Mom would measure everything, then put down piles of newspapers (which she had saved for weeks) for the underlining; then she would cut the oilcloth, hopefully right. Sometimes it would crack and break. That would be a disaster, for then she would have to start all over again, trying to hide the worst parts under a rug. No one ever had carpets, least of all fitted carpets.

Mom also bought brown vegetable bags for two pence. These she would bleach until they came beautifully white, and she would use them to make pillowcases and towels. My mom was an expert at making the best use of any item. She was a real miracle worker! She *had* to be, for otherwise we would have been much worse off.

When the sheets began to get worn in the middle, mom cut them through and then sewed the ends to the middle. It was very uncomfortable lying on the stitches (especially for Margaret, because she was the one who slept in the middle of the three of us). After a while when the sheets were worn beyond repair, mom still found many uses for the material. It would be used for dusters, dishcloths, floor cloths and handkerchiefs. When we got older large pieces of cloth were saved to make sanitary towels. These were re-used time and again, and though boiled would still have faint bloodstains which could have been either from my sisters or me. The cloths were put into the cupboard for all three of us to re-use.

Nothing, but nothing, was ever wasted in our home!

Once a week we had a special treat of fish and chips. The chips cost a penny and the fish three pence. We each had a portion of chips and one fish was shared between all of us. Sometimes the lady serving would give us a free bag of scratchings (the bits of batter). There was always a huge queue at that shop and sometimes, by the time I had been served, it was almost time to go back to school.

Next to the fish shop was the corner shop we didn't use very often for it was much cheaper to go to the market, but occasionally we *had* to call there. It was run by an elderly lady who was very fat. She was almost as fat as she was high. She was very slow at serving and we always knew we would be in that shop for ages. The shop only held about ten people who elbowed one another to get to the counter. She hated the door open and always shouted, "Shut the door!" to everyone who entered the shop. It became so full that the door would only open a few inches anyway. People had to turn and enter the shop sideways. The only time I ever saw that shop empty was when a mentally retarded boy went in with a list for his mother's shopping. Sometimes he would have a fit in there and people would be terrified and so ran away in all directions if he entered. The shopkeeper wore a large chain around her waist with a key attached, and each time she served anyone she went to a drawer, unlocked it, put in the money, took out the change, locked the drawer again, served the next customer and then repeated the whole process. It was when the shop got really full that the fun started, for she had to call into the back room for her daughter to come and help. She, in fact, was no help at all. For a start, there wasn't nearly enough room for two people behind that small counter. The daughter, who was no lightweight, had to squeeze and push past the mother. They got in each other's way and were always arguing. The mother would never release the key to the drawer, and when the daughter served anyone she had to wait until the mother had served her own customer before she opened the drawer. Then she had to give the money to her mother who would get a bit of paper and check the daughter's reckoning up to see if it was right before giving her the change—even though the daughter was well over Forty. It was hilarious—they were a great double act. (The TV soaps of today might have learned a great deal and got plenty of material from that corner shop!)

The mother kept a strap book which, again, was kept under lock and key; and again the daughter wasn't allowed anywhere near that book. People who hadn't any money in the week could strap until the weekend when they had to pay up.

I used to go to the shop for a bottle of lemonade for my brother Eric who was nine years older than me and was working, so had pocket money. The lemonade was two pence and a penny on the bottle. He always told me I could have the penny from the return of the bottle. He never gave me any of the lemonade, but when he gave me the empty bottle it meant I had two journeys before I had earned my penny. I also went to the shop for the neighbours. One lady was quite a bad offender at paying her bill. When she hadn't the face to go into the shop she would ask me to go in for her. In all innocence I would walk into the shop and ask for shopping for Mrs D, only to be told she couldn't have more credit until her debt was clear.

Sometimes I was in that shop so long I would take a book to read, standing up in the middle of the crush and letting the people behind push me forward towards the counter. I never needed any encouragement to read (which was just as well, for I never ever got any). I could, and did read anytime, anywhere, anyplace. Sometimes, though, I was inquisitively watching the old lady serving. If anyone wanted butter, I would give a groan because I just knew it would take her a long time to serve that customer. First she had to search for her large knife (which could be anywhere). When she finally found the knife she would wipe it clean on her apron, then cut a large slice from the slab of butter which would be all runny at the sides where the sun had caught it. She would weigh it, then put a bit more on, take a bit more off; each time she would have to walk from the shelf to the scales which were on the counter, still holding the butter between her fingers and the knife. She would bump into her daughter during her journey back and forth. Sometimes she had to remove her cat from where it was sunning itself on the shelf. If anyone wanted washing-bar soap, the same knife would be used, again with a wipe on the apron. It was used to cut cake, cheese, and many other things. I don't think there could have been many health regulations in those days, but if there were, that old lady was either unconcerned or blissfully ignorant about them! The shop had sticky flypapers hanging from the ceiling and kept there for days on end; often they were black with all the dead flies. Another of my occupations while waiting my turn to be served was counting the dead flies on those sticky strips of flypaper! (I've always had an obsession with counting!) I had to be careful not to be pushed too far forward into the sticky conglomeration of fly corpses or my hair would have been caught up in the horrid mess.

In that shop I learned many facts of life. I heard all the local gossip. The customers would lean forward and whisper into each other's ears while my interest would seem to be engaged elsewhere—but, my ears were sharp and I didn't miss much. They would snigger at a so-called 'premature birth,' remarking on just how quickly the nine months had fled since the wedding. The grapevine at that shop was spot on.

Wife swapping certainly isn't something new, I can tell you! That shop was always the first place to find out who was carrying on with another man's wife. Lots of the children had 'Uncles' and some couples that went drinking together often changed partners for the night once they had had a few beers. The children would wake up in the morning to find an 'Uncle' was in bed with their mom while their dad was elsewhere. My brother Bernard used to make up songs to the tune of Christopher Robin about the various couples and their carryings on—songs that were very clever and had us all helpless with laughter.

Towards Christmas the old lady ran a saving club. I used to pay a penny or two pence a week, depending on how good the horses were running and how flush I was with money. Cheap toys were displayed in the window along with sweets and boxes of chocolates. Choosing the things I wanted, or more importantly the things I could afford, was the hardest thing to do. I spent ages with my nose glued to that window! Often the old lady would bang on the window and tell me to clear off.

The only time we had chicken was for Christmas lunch and we would all help to remove the feathers—quite an arduous job that made our fingers sore. Mom would have to clear out the giblets from the inside of the chicken.

I had a great liking for chocolate drops, buying a pennyworth on my way to school; sometimes, though, I saved my penny until I got nearer to school, for there was an old house right next door to the school which had turned it's front room into a shop. The big heavy door had a bell that made a very loud noise when we went into the room. A lady would instantly come rushing through from the back room. The windowsills, the shelf over the fireplace, and an old kitchen table that served as a makeshift counter, were overflowing with sweets of all kinds. There were aniseed balls, liquorice laces, black jacks, sherbet dabs and of course my favourite chocolate drops. We would hither and dither for a long time in that shop until the lady got quite annoyed and told us to hurry and make up our minds. I would have to hurry to eat my chocolates before the school bell went. I always saved about four, which were for my mom. I would spend so much time debating whether or not to eat them that they became quite well handled, melting into one horrible blob inside of the bag. Most of the time I managed to resist the temptation and the sweets would stay in my pocket all day, and come home time I would be feeling quite pleased with myself and would then hand the whole mess to mom. She invariably scooped up the gooey mess and thanked me as she tucked into the melted horrible blob. I can think of no greater mother love than that.

7

Most of the tradesmen came up the street on a horse and cart or a three-wheeled tricycle. Those with the tricycles included the ice cream man, the man who sharpened knives and scissors, and the pikelet man.

When the ice cream man pedalled into view we would take out a glass and he would fill it to the top for a penny. The man who sharpened the knives and scissors also rendered his services for a penny a time. He pedalled like mad and the pedals would turn a chain which in turn had some sort of stone to sharpen the knives.

The pikelet man pedalled (and peddled!) up the street every Sunday afternoon calling out his wares. We ran out to buy two pennyworths of pikelets, which was enough for all our teas. We would take turns sitting by the fire with the long toasting fork, and when the pikelets were golden brown they were smothered in margarine which soon melted and ran down our chins. Lovely...lovely! I can taste them still.

The rag and bone man came round with a horse and cart, and quite regularly. I would run indoors, asking mom if we had any rags (which were well and truly rags by the time we'd finished with them). I always rushed indoors to get there before Margaret so I could have the goodies; sometimes, though, she got there before me, and then we would argue and fight over those few rags. In exchange for the rags the ragman gave cracked cups and saucers, or balloons we couldn't blow up because they were full of holes. We had to take a container full of water with us if we wanted goldfish. There were also day-old chicks that never lived for long. If there were any woollens amongst the rags, the ragman would ask if we wanted goods or a penny. I used to go for the money every time, but I wasn't too happy when mom made me share it with Margaret.

The scrap man also had a horse and cart. It was a red-letter day when *he* arrived. He would shout, "Any old iron!" and walk around the back garden to see if there was anything of value for him. It was great when he came for he gave two pence for the iron, or sometimes, on a good day, even three pence.

The greengrocer also had a horse and cart; so did the bread man, milkman, dustmen and the coal men. I used to follow them around several streets with a bucket and shovel, in the hope that the horses would leave their calling card so that there would be some manure for the garden. I would follow the coal cart for a much more valuable cargo than horse manure, for sometimes when the cart turned a corner bits of coal fell from the cart and I very quickly scooped these up into the bucket. I would be long away before the coal men realised their loss!

The only cars I ever remember coming up the street was when there was a general election and usually it was cars for the Tory party. The cars would be covered with Tory slogans. A loudspeaker would be blaring, "Vote Tory!" The people rushed out of their houses, gathered all their children and piled high into the cars for the free ride to the polling station—where they would vote Labour. They thought it was a great joke and had many a laugh and giggle about that.

I used to go to an outdoor off-license to get my dad's beer. The place was run by an old lady. It was for outdoor sales only, but in a corner she placed two stools that were for two old cronies to have their half pints. The stools were out of sight of the door and window, so if any policeman cycled by he wouldn't be able to see inside of the shop, for it was against the law to drink in an off-license. There always seemed to be lots of petty laws people always managed to get around somehow. We had to take our own bottle and the old lady had to put a sticker across the cork and the bottle: that was to prevent the children who were fetching the beer having a swig out of the bottle on the way home! I didn't like the taste of beer so I was never tempted.

There was a big jar of toffees on the counter and after we had been served the old lady would plunge her hand into the jar. I suppose it depended on her mood at a particular time as to whether she gave us one or more of the toffees.

One day I went with a two-shilling piece to get the beer and the old lady gave me change for half a crown. I was very good at reckoning up money, so of course I realised she had given me too much change—but I certainly didn't intend to let on that I knew. I felt pleased with myself with the extra sixpence in my sticky fingers. All the way home I planned just how I was going to spend that huge sum of money, for I had already made up my mind that it belonged to me. I was the one who had done the errand, after all, so, I reasoned it *had* to be mine!

When I reached home I couldn't keep my good news to myself. That was my big mistake, for my dad insisted on me taking it right back. I argued that the sixpence was mine, and when I failed to convince him of this I asked if I could take it back the next day. It was quite a long walk and it really annoyed me that not only was I losing the sixpence I already thought of as mine, but I had that extra long walk—and for nothing!

When I finally got back to the off-license and explained to the old lady that she had given me too much change, she was so pleased that she gave me an extra handful of toffees. I was taught a lesson in honesty that day, but I confess I still would rather have had the sixpence!

One of our neighbours was in regular work with good money, so he was financially better off than anyone else. Each payday he would push a half-crown piece (twelve and a half pence) through our letterbox. That was for dad who, owing to illness, wasn't at work very often. Dad regarded that as his pocket money and often would be waiting inside of the hall for the money to drop through the letterbox. The neighbour never mentioned the money.

In those days cigarettes never had filter tips—the cigarette was all tobacco. The neighbour was a heavy smoker who never smoked a cigarette right down to the end, so he used to put the 'dog ends' into a tin and his wife would bring the tin round to our house for dad, who would then take the tobacco from the dog ends and re-roll it on a little machine. Sometimes I re-rolled the cigarettes for dad, but the ends of the paper had to be licked together and I didn't like doing that. Old dog ends from cigarettes were always saved by people who were poor. I've seen old men searching the gutters for dog ends that had been thrown away by people who didn't have to count their pennies.

Every Sunday morning a man came round the houses for the peelings we kept in the coal house, but by the end of the week those peelings had began to smell quite horribly. We never knew the man, or where he came from, for there were no farms anywhere near to us; all we knew was that he kept pigs, and every Christmas morning he came round and gave everyone a pound of bacon.

Before Christmas I would get on my hands and knees and pray with all my might for the one thing I really ached for—a *beautiful red scooter*! Father Christmas just *had* to hear my prayers—yet all my prayers and longings fell on deaf ears for I never did get that scooter. (My granddaughter bought a red scooter for me sixty-five years later, but that's another story!)

My mom had a dread of getting into debt, and what she couldn't afford we simply didn't have. All the children in the neighbourhood came out to play on Christmas morning with their bikes, doll prams, doll pushchairs and big red scooters that had been bought on tick from the 'Tally man.' He called round every week for the instalments. Sometimes, when the women hadn't the money to pay him, they locked their doors and hid upstairs. He used to knock on the front door and look through the window, then walk round to the back door and bang on that and look through the kitchen window, thinking that perhaps they were hiding downstairs. He always knew they were hiding. He was as crafty as the women, for he would go away, wait until they came out of hiding, and then double back and catch them before they had a chance to hide again! If the money wasn't paid after a few weeks he would retrieve the goods, so it wasn't long before the toys disappeared from sight.

For Christmas we always had a stocking with an apple, orange, a few sweets, nuts and a three-penny bit. My elder sister spent hours making raffia baskets for us; she also made them for sale. We also had cut-out books with figures and clothes to dress.

I don't recall whether my knitted doll was a Christmas present or not. I do know, however, that it played a very important part in my life. It went everywhere with me. It shared all my secrets and witnessed my tears. I was always too shy to make friends, so the doll became my safety valve, my barrier against the knocks. My brother Bernard used to tease me unmercifully, snatching the doll from my arms and running outside with it. He would put his arms around its neck and tell me he was going to strangle it. He also hung it on the washing line until it became bigger and bigger. I screamed and cried for hours because I thought it could feel pain. *I* felt its pain, of course! I would punch and punch my brother to reach my doll, but he was older and much bigger than me. He would laugh and tantalise me by holding the doll just out of my reach. Maybe the neck stretching and the hanging was the reason the doll was about four times it original size! Although I had that doll for many years, it never did have a name.

I don't recall just what happened to my Confessor, my Companion and my friend. It must have outlived its usefulness. I hope I was kind to her at the end, for I know I loved her dearly. I still remember her with great affection—much more so, I'm sure, than my grandchildren will remember their bikes, televisions and computers.

A boy in our street who was about my age asked me if I would like to go and watch Walsall football team. He said I only needed the bus fare for both ways because he knew where the fence was broken and we could squeeze through. No doubt he had been there many times before! I saved the bus fare and we went on our great adventure, which was completely spoiled for me because I was terrified of being caught! That was the first and last time I have ever been to a football match!

8

We all had our jobs to do around the house. The one job I really hated was having to empty the chamber pots before I went to school! It was a vile job. The pots in my brothers' and our bedroom were enamel and I had to use scouring powder and a scrubbing brush, and really had to scrub away at them. My hands would get very sore! It was much worse emptying my dad's chamber pot which was platter. My dad had bronchitis and had to continually spit into the pot, and the green slimy phlegm would stick to the sides of the pot and I had to get some newspaper to clean it off. *I used to wretch doing that job!*

I also used to clean the cutlery, first covering the table with newspaper, then getting a bowl of warm water. I would rub the same scouring powder onto the cutlery which I would put into the warm water to rinse off before finally polishing. I would place the cutlery into the drawer in the table, then finally scrub the table.

I can remember cutting up newspaper squares, poking a hole to put the string through, then putting the string onto a nail which had been knocked into the toilet wall. The newspaper was much more interesting than toilet paper for I could read it while on the toilet! The main trouble, though, was that there was never a complete item of news on the small squares, so I had to use my imagination to make up the end of the stories. The toilet was plain brickwork painted white. I would stare hard at those bricks until patterns emerged. I could see faces, rivers, mountains and all manner of different things on that plain wall. It wasn't really a place to linger in for it was terribly cold in there. It was just outside of the back door and it was very draughty with a pane of glass missing from the window. Margaret had locked herself in the toilet when she was two years old and everyone had panicked until a neighbour broke the window and climbed in to reach her. The pane of glass had never been replaced. It was quite scary in there at night, especially with the back door closed; there wasn't any lights in there and I used to sing at the top of my voice, at the same time imagining I could hear ghostly footsteps coming up the path.

The council housing visitor would arrive unexpectedly to inspect the houses to see if they were kept clean. She never did house-to-house: she was much too crafty for that! Instead, she would visit one house up the top of the street, call into the next street and then double back into our street to visit a few more houses. She liked to keep people on their toes. Doing the visiting that way, she hoped to catch people out. But she reckoned without the grapevine! Ours was a close community and everyone looked out for one another. A neighbour catching sight of her would go up and down the street, warning everyone she was around. It was a great network. When we had been informed, everyone, including my brothers, would rush around and get cracking to do their allotted jobs.

It was all systems go. I would grab a duster, rush upstairs, and get under the beds to dust the oilcloth. My sisters would be dusting and sweeping up there with me. We would open the windows to shake out the dusters while mom and my brothers did a quick tidying downstairs. When the housing lady finally arrived she would glance around the living room, sit by the fire, have a cup of tea, then rest her weary legs. (Council officials didn't have cars in those days.) She would say, "I won't bother to inspect the upstairs today." I would wish we had known that earlier—it would have saved us all rushing about! She always knew, though, which houses were just untidy and which were the really dirty ones.

In some houses she would have a thorough check and be there for ages, looking under mats, checking cupboards, looking under beds and looking in every corner and cranny. When anyone was found to have a really filthy house she would give them a week to clean it up; and if after that week there was no improvement, they would be reported to the council. Although I don't recall anyone actually being turned out of their home, I do remember some houses being fumigated, which meant that the family had to be found alternative accommodation while the fumigation was being carried out. Every window and door was sealed for so many days. Even furniture was fumigated, and if it was considered too bad it had to be burnt. After a while the seals were taken off and the doors and windows left wide open for days to let out the fumes. The family would then be allowed back into the house with a very strict warning not to let it happen again or they would be out for good. After that the housing visitor would keep a very close watch on that family. They would be very shamefaced for ages afterwards, for resorting to fumigation was considered a great disgrace. The neighbours kept their distance from them and everyone would know about it. News used to travel like wildfire, for the grapevine was better than any jungle drum.

Mr Tooth the school inspector used to call around if we were away from school, and there had to be a good reason for the children's absence or their parents would be fined. If ever he saw us out during school time, it would mean big trouble! Several times I would see him before he saw me, and although I would have been away from school because of hospital visits, I would still be afraid and try to keep out of his sight. He was a very scary man.

The haircutting neighbour would save up all the coppers he received from his sideline and one week in the summer would take his family on holiday to Blackpool. They were the only family in the whole street that could afford a holiday, so their departure was quite an occasion for everyone in the street. Some of the neighbours got up early to see them off and even helped to carry their luggage to the railway station. Some of the people did, however, have a working holiday. During the school holidays they went hop picking for several weeks at a time. If the children weren't back in time for school, then the message would be that they had the measles—although the schools always knew it was "Hop picking measles." The children always came back looking well and as brown as berries, having spent many hours working in the hop fields in

Kent. They were always rigged from head to toe in new clothes from the hop picking money they earned. But they wouldn't be able to keep the new clothes for long. Sooner or later, when the money ran out, the clothes would end up in the pawnshop.

There was one family I remember who were much better off than anyone else; for a start, they were different from everyone else in that they only had the one child. The father was a long distance lorry driver. (I don't really think that was the reason for there being just the one child…although, on second thoughts, it *could* have been, of course.) Anyway, one day a car appeared outside their house and the lady of the house spent the entire day admiring the car. She lost no time at all in telling the whole street that the car belonged to her husband. No one else on the whole estate had a car. The news spread like wildfire! Every-one, but *everyone*, came to look at that car.

Some people were envious, some sarcastic. It was well and truly one up and above any Jones's that I knew of.

Sometimes on our school holidays we had a day out with my favou-rite aunt and my cousins. It was a real treat that we all looked forward to for days. We went up the Lickey Hills, which meant we had to go on the trams. That in itself was quite an adventure. I remember, once, while we were waiting in the queue, my cousin John got quite excited and pushed between a man and woman in the queue. The man grabbed hold of him and, pushing him back, said, "Son, never, but *never* get between a husband and wife!"

Mom and my aunt would make piles of sandwiches, buy bottles of lemonade, and we were away. We had many great days running and racing up the hills. We spent many happy hours running wild, going home tired, dirty and happy.

We had a silly old dog that would sit still while we dressed him up, putting a pair of old glasses on him. We would push him around in a truck that Bernard had made with bits of wood, old pram wheels and a rope for steering. The dog was quite content to be pushed around. (At least with his glasses on he could see where he was going!)

Once, when a neighbour called round to our house, my sister Jessie pretended she was going out. She said cheerio to the neighbour, then went through the kitchen into the passageway between the living room and the stairs. She went quietly up the stairs and searched the trunk that still held all of grandma's old clothes (we never threw anything away). She found a long dress which she managed to hitch up; she dragged out some old-fashioned shoes, a fox fur, pair of glasses and a big hat which she pulled low down her face. She then crept downstairs, again going through the passageway into the kitchen, out of the back door, round the side of the house and so to the front door. She knocked on the door and when mom answered she pretended to be a long lost relative.

She did this on more than one occasion and Mom always went along with the joke. She would express great surprise at seeing 'Aunt Bertha' after so many years, kissing, and making a big fuss of 'Aunt Bertha.' She would then introduce our Aunt to the neighbour. There was always quiet, polite conversation for a few minutes; then our neighbour would stand up and make some excuse for leaving, saying we needed some time alone with our visitor. 'Aunt Bertha' would say, "Please don't go because of me!"

One or another of us would burst into laughter, giving the game away. The neighbour would look in astonishment at us all, thinking we had all gone raving mad. Finally the penny would drop and the neighbour would realize Jessie had played a trick on her. She would exclaim, "You little bugger!" My sister might have been a very good actress.

All of us liked to dress up in grandma's clothes, but none of us was as good at getting everything just right as Jessie was. When Jessie was fourteen she brought home her first boyfriend, who was sixteen. He was an only child and very shy. His parents were separated, and he couldn't take my sister to his home because his mother was very jealous and possessive. She wanted to hold onto him, perhaps because of her own failed marriage. He was very apprehensive at meeting our family. He would have been much more so if he had known us! Nevertheless mom welcomed him into our family, as she did every one else who entered it. Because of his shyness both of my brothers gave him a really hard time. Bernard would pull out a chair for him and make him wait until Eric had fetched a duster; then they would both carefully dust the chair before letting him sit down. He would blush and never quite know what to say or do! The teasing would go on unmercifully with my brothers singing to him: "Little sir echo, how do you do?" They did this more so because the poor lad never used to say one word. He had red hair that seemed to show up much more when he blushed.

Jessie would get angry and very embarrassed by my brothers' behaviour and she would have a free for all with them. I just sat and watched all that went on. The boy would fidget and not know what to do. Then mom would come to the rescue and make my brothers behave. In spite of all the teasing the boy came back again and again, so he couldn't have thought we were too bad.

One day my sister and her boyfriend had a big argument. She told him not to call again, and that she didn't want to see him again. I was just as heartbroken as he was, for I hero-worshipped him. As he walked disconsolately down the street I ran after him and, clinging to his arm, I asked, "If my sister doesn't want you, can I have you instead?" I asked him to wait until I was grown up—then I could marry him. He replied that I was only eight years old and he didn't want to wait that long; and anyway, he pointed out, it was my sister he loved.

That was the first and only time I proposed to anyone! It certainly didn't do my ego much good to be rejected.

9

We had some rich relatives—rich to us, anyway. A cousin who was an only child, and who was much older than us, had been brought up in very different circumstances to our lifestyle. She married a very clever young man and they started their married life in a very old cottage next door to where her parents lived. Soon they were sufficiently well off to buy the cottage. After a while they bought the cottage her parents lived in (this was the time when it was unheard of for working-class people to buy their own homes). Then they bought the whole row of cottages! We couldn't fathom out how they could afford to buy one cottage, let alone a whole row! After that they bought and sold shops, getting richer with each sale. Then they bought a riding school. My mom couldn't understand just why they had bought the riding school when neither of them knew the first thing about horses. My cousin informed mom it wasn't important for them to know anything about horses because they could afford to pay people who did know.

As a young child my cousin was very fond of mom, so naturally she wanted to show her husband off to us, and at the same time show him how the other half lived. He was a very shy and unassuming young man, though my brothers thought he was a sissy. He certainly didn't give the appearance of being a very astute businessman. They came in a grand black car. (All cars were black in those days.) All the neighbours came running out of their houses to have a good nose and stood around peering inside the car. We kids dashed in and out of the house. We didn't want to miss any of the conversation, but at the same time we wanted to show off to the neighbours that the people with the car were our relations. After we had finished bragging we would run back indoors, for we didn't want to miss anything. They carried large suitcases into the house, which they then emptied. Inside were the husband's cast-off clothes; there were shirts, suits, coats and shoes for my brothers, while my cousin had brought her discarded dresses, blouses, skirts, coats and shoes for my sister. The clothes were too big for me, but that didn't stop me being nosy and having a good look.

My brothers and sister could hardly wait for them to go before they divided up the spoils.

Although my brothers thought the husband was a sissy, they were still glad enough to have his clothes shared out between them. One time, when my cousin and her husband visited, the conversation seemed to be halted with everyone looking at each other, waiting for someone to speak. Bernard soon got fed up and disappeared into the kitchen, where he searched under the sink for the black lead mom used to polish the fireplace; next, he pinched a big knucklebone from the dog. He then went upstairs via the passageway and searched through the chest were grandma's old clothes where kept. He soon found what he was looking for—several old and musty fox furs. He then stripped off completely naked, painted his face and body with the black lead, and placed the furs in the appropriate place to cover his modesty. Thus attired, he came downstairs via the passage into the kitchen. He then leapt into the living room, heading straight for our visitors. Beating his chest with one hand and waving the knucklebone with the other, he made horrible grunting noises and executed a war dance around our visitors. For a few moments they looked completely terrified—I don't think they had ever seen a redheaded cannibal before! They would have fled if he hadn't been between them and the door. It really startled them! They turned to mom for help but for once in her life she was completely baffled.

The look on everyone's face was a picture I'll never forget! Terror was plainly written on the faces of our guests and sheer amazement on mom's, followed by embarrassment, until her wonderful sense of humour took over. We all fell about laughing and our visitors must have thought they had arrived in a madhouse. Then, luckily, they saw the joke! It certainly broke the ice: after that everyone was talking all at once. I realised, then, that although our cousin was much better off than us financially, we had so much more than she did: we had a close happy family and, although we had our troubles, we always clung together.

We were 'us'—and anyone outside of our immediate family were 'them.'

The main ingredient, the most essential thing to have in those hard times, was a sense of humour—which, fortunately, we all possessed.

After that episode my cousin and her husband came regularly, and when they left the husband always shook hands with mom and somehow a pound note always moved from his hand into mom's without anyone else noticing. He was a real gentleman and he became quite fond of our family once he got to know our ways.

Sometimes my uncle and aunt came with them. Then the atmosphere would be totally different, for my uncle was a terrible bore. He had had a stomach operation, and he always insisted on telling us all the gory details, whether we wanted to hear them or not. He would show us the operation scar as though it were a badge of honour. Mom would politely listen to him though it was very hard for her to keep a straight face, since both my brothers would be standing behind him and demonstrating with their own bodies just where the scar was. They would be miming his every word, for they had heard the story so very often that they were word perfect! My cousin would fall about in laughter. We were poor, but life was never dull in our family—especially when my brothers, who were both great comics, were around.

Mom kept all of our family treasures at the top of the cupboard. We weren't allowed to touch anything up there, so naturally as soon as mom went shopping I would drag the old horsehair sofa to the cupboard, place a chair on top, then wobbling about and holding the door with one hand, I would reach the articles down with the other. There was a wooden idol that a great uncle had brought from Africa, and beautifully embroidered greeting cards my uncle had sent from France during the first war. There was also a German officer's helmet with a spike on the top. The officer's name and rank were written inside of the helmet. My uncle had removed the helmet from a body on the battlefield of the First World War. Why he had given it to us and why it was at the top of our cupboard for many years I will never know. I would look at that helmet, often trying it on my head and wondering just what the person it had once belonged to had looked like. Did he have any family and did they know just how he had died? I was very glad I was too young to know the full history of that German soldier and his helmet.

There was a wooden box in which were kept old photos, birth certificates, rent books going back several years, insurance books, policies and all the papers to do with our family. I really got a great kick being nosy and going through that box! Best of all I never knew how long mom would be out shopping, and just how long I had to explore all the documents. It added to the excitement, knowing that at any moment I could get caught. That box is now in my possession, still doing its job of guarding my family's papers. However, looking through it, legitimately, now, whenever I feel like it, it doesn't give me the same pleasure and excitement I received when I reached up to that cupboard when I was a child!

We saved all our money before our school holidays to pay the bus fare to Walsall Arboretum. It was the nearest thing to the countryside that we had. It was a beautiful place with acres and acres of trees, and lovely flowers of all colours and smells. I didn't know the names of any of them, but to me that wasn't important, for I could, and did, appreciate their great beauty. There were lots of exotic birds. Peacocks strutted up and down, as if aware of all the admiring looks from the many people who took pleasure from their fine feathers and great haughtiness. There were lakes where people could hire boats just for a few pence and row for an hour. We didn't have any money to spare, so it wouldn't matter to us if it cost pence or pounds for the hire of the boats. I did, however, have my imagination: I stood and watched for ages, thinking how lucky those people were who could afford the cost.

In my imagination *I* would be rowing (or better still, allowing someone else do the rowing while I casually trailed my fingers through the water; naturally, a handsome young man would be sitting at my side). None of us could swim, anyway, so it was just as well for us that we left the lakes to the moorhens, ducks, swans and all other creatures whose natural habitat it was.

There was always a brass band playing, with the musicians looking very smart in their newly pressed uniforms and their highly polished shoes. I would find a sloping grassy area, sit down and get comfortable and then soak up the music. The sun on my face, the music in my ears—it was my idea of Heaven! I even put aside my books so that all of my concentration could be given to the music, the sunshine, and especially to the great feeling of happiness and sense of well being.

I sat there for hours until the rumbling of my stomach reminded me of another of my great loves—Food!

Going back to the subject of mom and the rest of the family, we spread a tablecloth on the grass and emptied the shopping bags we all had taken turns to carry, and which we had left with mom to mind while we had gone exploring. Now, though, only food was on all our minds! Out came the bread, margarine, cheese, tomatoes, eggs, and salmon paste (which mom had paid two pence a quarter of a pound for, and was for special occasions only). Out would come the large bread knife, and we would all watch mom cutting through the loaf. We grabbed a slice of bread almost before it was sliced through, making our sandwiches of whatever we wanted, and then swilling the lot down with lemonade.

It was nectar!

When we had finished eating, we cleared all the debris away, had a rest to let the food go down, then indulged in a game of football, using the now empty shopping bags as goal posts. It was during one of those games when the heel came off mom's shoe. We all chased around looking for a large stone so that she could hammer it back on, but to no avail. The heel stubbornly refused to be repaired. Not even mom's great inventiveness worked this time and she had to spend the rest of the day hobbling around. The heel was carefully placed into the shopping bag so she could repair it properly when she reached home. Whether she succeeded or not, I don't recall; but I do know she would have had a very good try. She had to find a way of mastering most things—especially if it made life that little bit easier for us all. (I still have the last which mom used to mend all our shoes.)

One day a neighbour called round our house to ask mom if she could borrow some pegs and a shopping bag. Mom invited her in, made a cup of tea, and they sat by the fire nattering away. While the neighbour was drinking her tea, she suddenly said that I had given her son a rabbit punch, and that I was spiteful! Mom replied that I was no more spiteful than any of the other children. With that the neighbour jumped up and threw the bag and pegs back at mom, saying, "She didn't want to borrow them anymore!" Mom replied, "Get out of my house, you stupid woman!"—or words to that effect!

There was one couple from our area I remember quite clearly. They must have been the only couple on the whole estate that were childless. They had the grandest house, the fanciest lace curtains, and the most beautiful garden at a time when other people couldn't afford the time, money or the energy on gardens. They never had second, third or fourth-hand furniture like everyone else, but brand new. Not that anyone was allowed in their home to see what it was like, but we all knew everyone's business. (There wasn't any television to occupy our interest in those days!) Anyway, a furniture van arriving in the district with brand new furniture was a very rare occurrence; it was enough to draw people from their houses, and to stand and have a good natter while they admired the new goods that were being delivered. We all knew the husband wasn't allowed to smoke indoors—he had to go down the garden for a sly smoke. (The macho men in the area despised him for that.) He wasn't allowed to walk in the house with his shoes on; he had to change into his slippers just outside of the back door. The wife was very house proud and kept things to herself, not mixing or chatting to neighbours. I don't know if they were childless by the fault of fate, or whether it was by design. I do know, though, that there was no love or happiness in that household. The wife had a full-time job, which was very unusual in those days. It was especially unusual for a married woman to go out to work if she didn't have children and therefore didn't need the extra wage. The men at that time didn't approve of their wives working, for it was regarded as a great slur on their manhood if they couldn't support their family on their weekly wage packet; so most men wouldn't hear of their wives going out to work, even if they desperately needed the extra money. The very few wives who did work always insisted it was only "pin money." There was no way a Black Country wife could earn as much or more money than her husband—that would have been a real blow to a man's pride. In most cases the poorer a family, the more macho was the head of the household.

This couple, however, didn't seem to have much communication with each other and they went their separate ways. Anyway, one day the wife went to work as usual, fell ill and promptly dropped down dead. Later, when the husband was going through her belongings, perhaps stepping into her bedroom for the first time in years, he opened a dressing-table drawer and discovered, to his great astonishment, hundreds of unopened wage packets. Some dated back more than twenty years! Needless to say, he lost no time enjoying his ill-gotten gains and soon introduced his lady friend into his home. The sterile relationship of that couple amounted to a complete loss of two people's lives, for divorce, for poor people, was practically unheard of in those days.

I only ever remember going to the dentist once as a child. It was one of the rare occasions when my dad was well enough to go out. Dad, in any case, went with me. I think I had several teeth out. I remember he gave me a penny because I didn't cry.

Mom used a cigarette holder to pull out her teeth. She would wedge her tooth into the hole where the cigarette should have been, then, when it was firmly in place, she would give it a twist. The tooth came out inside of the holder. Goodness knows where she got that cigarette holder from, for she never smoked a cigarette in her life!

Dad always used the pliers to pull out *his* teeth. He would twist and turn the pliers; then there would be a loud cracking noise and the tooth would come out in bits. So he had to do it again and again. Each time he would grimace with pain, his face getting greyer and greyer. I don't know how much the dentist charges were in those days; however much it was, my parents couldn't afford to pay for themselves. I don't recall whether there was a charge for children or not. If there were it would have taken a lot of scrimping and saving on my mom's part to pay for all of us. We never had toothbrushes and used to clean our teeth with a wet rag dipped in salt, and sometimes we used soot from the fire grate. Strangely enough, I had very good teeth. Maybe that was because we couldn't afford to eat many sweets, although I remember I used to lick my fingers and then dip them into the sugar bowl, then shake the sugar bowl to get rid of the telltale finger marks. For breakfast we had 'Ducks,' which was bread and margarine soaked in tea. That sounds revolting now, but at least it meant we had something warm inside us before we went to school. There was no fancy breakfast cereals, or money to pay for them if there had been.

For some strange unknown reason I liked to drink the boiled cabbage water. The idea of that fills me with horror now, but mom used to save a cup full of the stuff, and I would relish it. None of my brothers and sisters ever wanted the cabbage water; they probably thought I was mad.

A boy in Bernard's class would make my life a misery, calling me 'Cock eyes or four eyes' whenever he saw me. One day he threw an apple core at me. It hit me in the face and I went home crying. Bernard didn't say a word. He just got up and went outside looking for the boy. He gave the boy a good hiding, causing him to be knocked out cold when his head hit the kerb. The boy had to be carried home and caused quite a commotion in the street. That boy was always very nice to me after that.

My brother thought it was quite in order for him to tease me, but he wouldn't allow anyone else to do so.

10

Although I was only nine when war was declared, I remember that day very well. Mom and dad sat all day anxiously listening to the wireless. "We are now at war," the Prime Minister announced. Although I didn't understand just what all the fuss was about, I knew it was something very, very serious. The pain, sadness and unhappiness on my parents' faces left me in no doubt about that.

Eric had recently joined the Territorial Army and had gone on a fortnight's training. His eighteenth birthday occurred during that fortnight. He was due home the day war was declared. My dad stood at the gate, just staring down the street and willing my brother to turn the corner into the street. It was to no avail, as I'm sure my dad well knew. My brother didn't turn that corner into our street until many months later. By that time the cheeky, lively young boy with lovely wavy ginger hair had changed into a serious young man with short-cropped hair.

So began a very sad time for everyone. Food, clothes, furniture and coal all became rationed. Clothes being rationed, though, were the last things to worry us. We had always had to make do, so it was no hardship for us. Soon after the war started women had to do some war work. Mom started an evening job in a local factory. She soon made many friends. One of the women she became friendly with only had the one child—a daughter in her teens (although no-one was called a teenager in those days). The young girl had been used to having lots of new clothes, and her mother had always catered for her every whim. Now, though, with the start of rationing and the issuing of clothing coupons, a limit was soon put to her large wardrobe—though not for very long.

We had never, but *never* had new clothes. So mom and her friend devised a smart plan. The workmate would have most of our clothing coupons (which we couldn't afford to use anyway). In return, we had the daughter's discarded clothes, which after all were only second-hand by the time we received them. I recall mom coming home with the very large bundle of clothes, which was shared out between us, although most of the clothes were too big for Margaret and myself. My elder sister Jessie was quite happy with the arrangement for she got the lion's share.

There was a flourishing black market. Money, then as now, always spoke loud and clear. There were eating places called British restaurants where people could eat out without using their food coupons.

People with money could, and did, get away with anything that didn't apply to us. We had no money—period! Nevertheless, like everyone else at that time, we thought up some crafty moves to try to make life that little bit easier for us all. Tea, sugar, cream, butter, meat and petrol became rationed in 1940. Cheese, clothes, jam and shell eggs went on ration the following year. Powdered eggs could be bought without coupons: each family was allowed one packet a week, but I seem to remember that it tasted vile.

Oranges were for expectant mothers only. Each person was allowed one pound of onions a week, but people who grew their own were requested not to buy onions. Everyone was urged to grow his or her own vegetables.

We seemed to manage quite well with our food coupons each week. Rations varied throughout the war according to the supply. The following quotes the lowest rations per person per week in 1944:

Cheese—one ounce; cooking fats, tea and butter—two ounces; margarine, bacon, and ham—four ounces; sugar—eight ounces.

Offal was unrationed and was usually available under the counter for favourite customers.

The points value was: rice, sago, tapioca, dried fruits—two points; baked beans, cereals and biscuits—four points; condensed milk, canned fruit—eight points; luncheon meat and sardines—sixteen points.

Soap was also rationed. We could have either toilet soap or flakes—three ounces; hard soap—four ounces; soft soap and soap powder—six ounces.

Each man, woman, and child was allowed sixty-six clothing coupons a year.

Women's clothing rations were as follows:

Lined Macs or coats (over 28 inches long)—fourteen points. Dress, gown, frock, jacket, or short coat—eleven points. Gym tunic, skirt with bodice, pyjamas—eight points. Skirt—seven points. Nightdress—six points. Blouse, sport shirt, cardigan, jumper, slippers, shoes and boots—five points. Petticoat, slip, combinations, cami-knickers—four points. Undergarments including corsets, apron or pinafore—three points. Scarf, gloves, stockings, muffs, gloves or mittens—two points. Pair of ankle socks—one point.

Children's clothing points were slightly less than the women's and men's; more, for example, were men's shoes—seven points.

There was a great deal of propaganda from the government asking people to save.

The President of the board of trade, Hugh Dalton, made a speech thanking the women of the country, saying, "To all of you who have so cheerfully made do, who have mended and managed and got months of extra wear out of your own, your husband's and your children's clothes, I say thank you. Remember that every clothing coupon unspent means less strain on the country's resources. To wear clothes that have been patched and darned perhaps many times is to show oneself a true patriot. The 'Right' clothes are those we have worn for years, and the wrong ones are those we buy when we don't need them. Making do at times may seem a little dreary. Nearly every woman, and some men, would like something new to wear. But, even when old clothes aren't exciting, they are in a way a winning fashion, to follow which will speed the day of victory."

Hooray! Hooray! Hooray! So that was what we had been all our lives—true patriots without even knowing it! The rest of the country was being urged to make do and mend. My mom could have told the government of that day that making do and mend was more than "A little dreary"—it was survival. Perhaps people like my mom should have been in the government. They could have taught the government a thing or two. I found that speech very patronising and it seemed ironic to me that the people throughout the whole countryside were being told to pinch and scrape, to save and salvage, to do things my mom and thousands of other women had had to do all their lives just so that they could provide their children with the next meal! Mom and I used to stand in one queue for about a quarter of an hour before mom would move on to another queue while I kept her place. She would ask someone to keep her place in the second queue, and then double back when our first place was near to the counter. After we had been served, mom would find her place in the second queue and some-how she always managed to take me with her; that way we managed to get two helpings of the food that wasn't rationed.

We certainly weren't on our own in doing this! Everyone was up to all sorts of dodges. My mom and I often stood and waited for an hour or more for a quarter pound of tomatoes each. The tomatoes were for my dad who by this time was very ill. He worried a great deal about my brother. We didn't receive many letters from him, and those we did receive were censored. My mom went through a terrible time trying to keep bad news from dad and worrying about us all. Although my younger brother Bernard was too young to enlist, he was very keen to join the navy. Before coal became rationed we used to have to fetch it by the barrow load. It was four old pence for twenty-eight lbs. 'Mrs such-a-thing' would come running and tell us when the coal man had a delivery. Then it was all systems go! Out would come the barrows, carts, old prams, in fact anything that had wheels which would enable us to get the coal home. The coal man didn't have to do any deliveries, for as soon as there was a whisper that the coal had arrived at the depot, people would form a long queue. Bernard and I would get our contrap-tions on wheels and make our way to the depot. We would be shivering with cold as we made several journeys backwards and forwards, each of us pulling or pushing our weird vehicles that held our precious cargo.

Sometimes my brother and I would search round the old mining areas. We used to go to an area called "The Shit and Alley." Why it was called that I never knew. We also searched on a big waste tip for anything that would burn. It was a dangerous thing to do because the rubbish would move under our feet and we would often fall back to the bottom of the tip. We must have thought it worth the effort. Often there would be Bakelite boxes on the tip that everyone scrambled to find and almost fought for. Those boxes could be filled with wet slack and they sent out quite a warm glow; the trouble was, though, that the Bakelite would make loud sizzling noises and then spit out in all directions, so that someone had to be on hand at all times to quickly put the embers back onto the fire. We had to put up with all kinds of nuisance just to keep warm.

On the stroke of midnight New Year's Eve one of our neighbours (who tradition said had to be a dark-headed man) would arrive at our front door, then sing in the New Year. We had to wait until he had finished the song before opening the door to let him in. In his hands he always carried a small piece of coal and a slice of bread. He would then walk around the table, put the coal on the fire and the bread on the table. This was a symbol that the household would have food and warmth for the following year. We all waited and watched until he had wordlessly finished his task. Then he would pick up the full glass that had been prepared before his arrival, toast our family's good health, empty the glass, and walk all round the table again before leaving by the back door. It was considered unlucky to go out of the same door he came in. We all had to wait until that ritual was completed before we could go to bed.

Eric came home on leave a few times before he went abroad. He looked very smart in his khaki uniform. He was a very good-looking young man and had lots of girl friends. Once he brought an A.T.S girl home with him. I remember my dad telling the girl off because she was smoking at the meal table, and she threw the cigarette butt right across the table onto the fire while we were all still eating! That was one liaison that didn't last for long. When Eric went back after his leave the house seemed very quiet without him. He always brought a special service ration book which allowed service men much more rations than civilians and was issued to all service men on home leave. The sweets rations for everyone was just two ounces each. We always put all our coupons together and had a big bag of an assortment of different sweets we shared out between us. My family was silly enough to let me choose and fetch the sweets! Naturally I always chose my own favourites, and somehow there would always be a few less sweets in the bag before I reached home. I was only nine years old, after all, and the temptation was very great.

With Eric in the army, it meant even less money coming into the house. Dad hadn't been able to work for years: he was on some kind of means test, which by now was the bare minimum—I think it was about ten shillings a week. Although dad was near pension age, my sister and I were both under ten. I don't think that was ever taken into consideration by the means test people.

Life was certainly a constant struggle. Jessie had turned sixteen and she earned about two pounds a week. She was the main breadwinner for the family, and even with mom's part-time earnings, it was still a problem to make ends meet. I don't know how my mom managed. Life must have been one struggle after another for her, although she always found ways of making little treats for us.

At school part of the playground and part of the churchyard was dug up to make the air raid shelter. It was built in a circle, and there were no lights or seats. We all had to march round and round, with our hands on the shoulders of the child in front of us. Each teacher had a torch or a candle, and would lead their class. We had to sing as we marched along. I seem to remember that it was mainly hymns we had to sing at the top of our voices. (It seems ironic to me that we had to sing hymns while men of the same religion were flying enemy planes and dropping bombs above us.) I remember I was always more scared of the graves that were only a few feet away than I was of the German planes overhead. I always let my imagination work overtime. Indeed, I was petrified, almost expecting to stumble over some dead body that had accidentally been disturbed during the making of the shelter. If I had been allowed to choose, I think I would have preferred taking my chances above in the playground!

We always knew by the sound of the planes whether they were the enemy's or ours. We also knew by the heaviness of the noise whether they had dropped their bombs, or were still loaded. It was a scary time. We children always searched the streets after a raid for shrapnel—the bits of metal that had broken off from the shells. The German planes were aiming mainly for the Old Parks work and for all the other many ammunition factories in our area. We had to queue for hours to be fitted with gas masks. It always seemed to me that we spent a great deal of our lives queuing. Everyone seemed so patient; the main cry was always, "There's a war on: everyone, even children, must do their bit!" We were hardly likely to forget about the war with the constant reminders and our awful lifestyle.

An air raid warden had the gas masks for the whole area delivered to his home. The queue for the masks stretched into four streets: we would move a few steps, then stop, move a few more steps, then stop again. We shuffled along in this manner, it seemed to me, forever, until we finally arrived at the garden gate; still in an orderly queue, we would then move along the garden path until we reached the front door. We then shuffled through the hall into the living room, where there were thousands of gas masks of all shapes and sizes piled high. The worst of all were the masks for babies, which were really weird. The babies had to be put inside of the mask. The babies would be terrified and scream non-stop, their mothers' terribly upset. Young children were crying, us older children trying very hard not to cry. Fathers were getting very impatient while the older people couldn't understand just what was going on. There must have been at least a dozen children wanting the toilet at the same time.

After we had been fitted with our masks we went through the kitchen and out of the back door. Thousands of people passed through that small council house during those few days. It must have been left in a terrible mess. That air raid warden and his wife (whose house it was) should have had a medal each—they certainly deserved them.

We had to carry our gas masks everywhere we went, and we were well drilled in what to do: if the sirens sounded on our way to school, we had to run to the nearest house and go down that shelter. If we hadn't gone too far, we turned and went back home. Every home had their back gardens dug up and an Anderson shelter put there. In ours there were four bunk beds and a small cabinet where we kept the first aid kit. On top of that stood two plates with candles, while a box of matches was always kept in exactly the same place at all times—so that mom would know just where she could put her hands on them in the pitch dark. There was always food taken down in case we were there for some time. A couple of chairs were placed between the bunk beds. A chamber pot was taken down too, in case of emergency. My mom was always prepared for any eventuality.

I always had plenty of reading matter down there, and would get as near to the candles as possible to have enough light to read by. It probably didn't do my eyesight much good, reading in the flickering light. Our shelter seemed to get quite crowded, for sometimes our neighbours came in with us for the company, and of course our dog was down there with us. We managed in spite of the crush, however. We slept (or tried to sleep) down that shelter for several months. I remember that it was very damp and unspeakably uncomfortable.

11

At school the nurse would come and inspect our hair to see if it was clean. She also measured our feet—that was a time I hated and really dreaded, because any child whose feet were size three or over were allowed ten extra clothing coupons. There were a couple of boys who qualified. I had size four shoes and I was the only girl in the whole class who received those coupons! I would cringe with embarrassment. It meant, though, that we could give mom's workmate the extra coupons in exchange for clothes. I would have preferred not having the coupons, for I was a scared, insecure child who hated having any attention drawn to her. I was happy only when I could be alone somewhere quiet with a book.

One day we heard on the grapevine that a butcher was selling offal to anyone. A queue quickly formed which my mom and I soon joined. We were both lucky and managed to get some liver—dad's favourite. Mom decided we would have liver and onions for our evening meal. The marvellous aroma of the meal being cooked wafted up to my nostrils, but when mom put my meal in front of me I couldn't touch it! For some reason or another I was in a dreadful mood. I don't recall the reason for my bad mood, but while it lasted I wouldn't eat or speak to anyone. I would just sit and glare at everyone; even my brother got the message and left me alone when I had what he called "the steely glint" in my eyes. My meal was always left just where it had been placed until my temper abated. No one else was allowed to touch it until I had cooled down; then I would eat the meal, even if it had gone cold. That particular evening my sister had been out somewhere and she didn't know I had been in one of my tempers. She walked in, looked at my plate, and said, "Don't you want that liver? Shame to waste it! Great! I'll have it!"

Before I or anyone else could stop her, she had picked up the liver and eaten it. I jumped up, forgetting for the moment that I wasn't speaking to anyone, and screamed out: "That's *my* liver! You've eaten my bloody liver!"

Everyone except me fell about laughing! I didn't see the funny side of it. In our family that story has been recalled many times, and was known as 'the floating liver.' The funny thing, though, is that I've never eaten liver since.

Although my sister was only sixteen, she was bringing in most of the money for the family. She worked all day in a factory and then some nights she would come home, have her tea and go straight back to the factory to do her turn of fire watching. She still had to work hard the following day. It was a terrible and unreal life for a sixteen-year-old.

Although I had missed quite a good deal of schooling, owing to all my hospital visits, I still came top of the class. The dreaded Headmistress called me out in front of the whole school at assembly. I was literally shaking in my shoes, fearful that she was going to ridicule me again and make me try to say the letter F—and this time it would be the whole school, not just one class, that would be laughing at me cringing with embarrassment. I was really terrified—I just couldn't stand being laughed at.

I still remember, even now, the great fear and hatred I had for that woman! She made my life hell; she destroyed my self-esteem, my confidence in myself, which was unforgivable. It was many, many years before I regained any regard for myself. It is only since the great urge to write took hold of me that the anger and pain within me found an avenue for release. This time, though, she didn't want to ridicule, but to praise.

I well remember, still with great anger, the sarcasm with which she announced that she would follow my career with interest—since she well knew, as I certainly did, that with our family circumstances there would never be the least chance of a career for me. She didn't even bother to put me down for a scholarship, regardless of the fact that I was top of the class. She had pigeonholed me because, in her eyes, I belonged to a poor working-class family; and in the nineteen thirties and forties you had few if any opportunities to better yourself if you were at the bottom of the pile, whether you were clever or not. You had to know your place.

I really wish, now, that the frightened, intimidated young girl who was me all those years ago, the girl who was frightened of her own shadow, was able then to find the courage to stand up to that screwed-up old bat who was incapable of understanding any child, and tell her just what she thought of her. I wish I had told her that I would always remember her malice. Instead, I just stood there, shaking, while she made a big play of giving me a prize—a silver three-penny bit. Even then, to me, it was far too little far too late. It couldn't undo all the harm and pain she had put me through. I would have loved to have thrown that three-penny bit right back into her spiteful face; but, of course, I was much too scared of her to do that, and to my great shame and anger I had to accept that humiliating "Prize." All of eleven years old, I walked out of the school gates for the last time and vowed that some day I would be back! Then I would show her just what I could do. (It was fifty years later, after she had been long dead, that I kept that vow—but that's another story!) Once out of the school gates I threw that three-penny bit as far as I could, even though to me it was a lot of money at the time. It could never be enough, in any case, to solve my pain and make things come right for me.

Lots of the other children with lower exam marks than me went on to grammar or high school. I knew that destiny wasn't for me—the cards were stacked too high. I knew that my mom could never afford to pay for school uniforms and bus fares, so I didn't even bother to tell her I had come top and could have gone on to grammar school; there was no point in giving her anymore worry. There was no financial help at all in those days, and my mom's greatest priority was to provide her children with the next meal. You either had the money or you didn't—and we certainly didn't. I also knew there was no chance at all of my staying at school until I was sixteen, although that was my dream and I desperately wanted to. That was out of the question and it was my misfortune that I was intelligent enough and old-headed enough at the great old age of eleven to appreciate this. From that time on I never made the least effort at school. I don't remember ever having any encouragement to do so; not once, in the whole of my short, painful childhood did anyone ever mention job prospects, careers, or ask me what I wanted to do when I left school. The Black Country certainly didn't have the elite of teachers in the Thirties and Forties. Nevertheless, for my own pride I always made sure that I did enough work to keep me in the 'A' stream; my stubborn pride wouldn't allow me to do anything less.

It was a great shock to us all when my aunt suddenly upped and left my uncle. They had always visited us every Sunday night, and had always seemed happy together. It was the first time anything like that had happened in our family. We were all curious to know the whys and wherefores—well, I was anyway! We never *did* find out. No other person was involved. My mom, being the person she was, decided to take another lame duck under her wing—she did my uncle's washing and ironing. Work shirts and trousers had to be scrubbed by hand. It was very hard graft. She would put the clean washing in a basket and I had to take it to his home each Sunday morning and bring back the dirty washing. For all that hard work mom was paid five shillings, and he gave me a three-penny bit. I used to ask my sister to come with me, and even offered her half of the money—but she didn't like my uncle and wouldn't come with me. I would ask the little girl next door. Sometimes she was able to come, but other times she had to visit her grandma and I had to go alone.

That was the time I dreaded!

When I arrived at my uncle's house he would have a beer bottle in his hands. He would be waiting for me to go to the off-licence to fetch his beer; then he would take the clean clothes and put the dirty clothes in the basket. He always gave me a glass of milk, and then he would give me the money. But when I was ready to leave he would reach out and pull me onto his lap, and his hands would be all over the top part of my body.

I can't honestly remember whether he told me not to tell anyone or not, but I knew even then that if I had told my mom she would have torn him and his washing to shreds. *I realised that fact.* I also knew that would mean that there would have been five shillings a week less coming into the home—*money we couldn't afford to lose.* I knew also it would cause great distress to my mom and she had more than her share of troubles. So, although I was terrified, I kept quiet and told no one...

In fact, it was a secret I kept locked up tight inside of me for over fifty long years—until one day I was with my two daughters and somehow the subject of child abuse came up. *I suddenly burst into tears.* For one split second my two most articulate daughters were completely speechless; then they both jumped up at the same time and put their arms around me. All three of us cried and cried. They sat with me while I poured out all my anger and pain. The great relief I felt telling my daughters of my fifty-year-old secret was tremendous. It was like a heavy load that was at last lifted from my shoulders. My daughters will never know how much they really helped me that day—just being there and letting me cry and listening to my distress. I thought long and hard about putting that unhappy episode into my story. At times I decided that it would go in, at others that it wouldn't. It has been a hard and touchy decision to make—one that has taken courage, but I realise it was part of my life, part of my childhood. I had to be perfectly honest with myself before I could open the floodgates.

It would please me very much if in the future anyone who has been abused reads my story and it helps them to speak to someone; believe me, opening the floodgates does help to finally take away the pain.

Also, I know that by writing about—by sharing—all the pain, bewilderment, and anger of my Black Country childhood, I am better equipped to face the future, and can encourage others to do the same. Each chapter has removed the pain, one brick at a time; and now, with this chapter, I have finally knocked down the very last brick of the great defensive wall I built around myself as a child.

12

Mom used to do all the painting and decorating for another aunt. After about three days hard graft, my aunt would give mom ten shillings. She usually gave her a horrible clay figurine, saying, "It's not the gift—it's the thought that counts." She didn't show much thought in exploiting a member of her own family—one whose financial position wasn't nearly as good as hers.

Then there was another aunt I liked, and understood. She didn't care in the least about housework. It didn't matter to her if the place was a mess, or if she had pretty flowery wallpaper or plain walls—but she did love her music. She had a large collection of Caruso records she would play all day long. I used to sit on the not too clean floor and listen to that great voice. My aunt would show me the records and explain the music to me. I would learn, and soak up the beautiful music. That, to me—and my aunt—was so very much more important than dusty furniture.

At home we had an old gramophone that had to be wound up. Goodness knows where it came from! We only had the one record, which was *The laughing Policeman*. After that record had been played a few hundred times the novelty began to wear off. Margaret and I would take it in turns to sit on the gramophone while the other wound it up, and in this way we would try to spin round on it. Naturally the machine couldn't take that punishment for long.

The senior school I moved to at eleven years of age had nine classes altogether—three at A level, three at B level and the other three at C level. I don't honestly think I learnt anything at all in the three years I was at that school. My teacher in 'IA' was a middle-aged spinster: she was tiny, very thin and had a yellow complexion—a nondescript person who was ill and away from school a great deal of the time. When she was away we had no teacher at all, for there weren't any supply teachers then. When she was there everything seemed too much trouble for her. I believe she was like me in wanting to get through the day without too much hassle. I was bored out of my mind that first year.

In those days we only had the one teacher for all the lessons, so if the teacher was mediocre it meant a wasted year, for it meant she was mediocre in all of our lessons. I managed to get through that first year without any effort on my part at all. I began to look forward to the long summer holiday and to the thought of going back to school into another class—and, much more importantly, moving up to '2A' and having a new teacher, perhaps one who would have some life in her, someone who could teach and regain my interest and respect.

When the new term began I walked into the new classroom feeling quite confident and happy, only to receive an unhappy and unpleasant surprise when the door opened and the same teacher walked in! For some unknown reason she had been moved up a class with us! I think that was the time I gave up on that school. About three years later I heard she had died. She must have been very ill all the time she was still working, poor woman. But poor us—the children who lost out on those two wasted years.

The teacher in '3A' was fair, fat and forty—the jolly hockey-stick type! I kept my head down and, fortunately for me, I wasn't one of her favourites. Her Christian name began with the letter F and she would say, "I know you girls think my name is Fanny, but my name isn't Fanny—Ha Ha Ha!" I couldn't have cared less what her name was. Nevertheless I didn't appreciate anyone making fun of *that* name, for it was my mom's and my grandmother's name—although my mom didn't like her name. Mom was the fourth daughter and she couldn't understand just why her parents hadn't named either one of her elder sisters after *their* mom. I was also the fourth daughter, and although I loved my mom dearly, I was very glad she named me Kathleen and not Fanny the third!

Throughout the three years I was at that school, one of my cousins was in the same class as me, although none of the children or the teachers knew of our relationship. Maybe my cousin didn't want her friends to know of her poor relation, and I was much too proud to say anything. My cousin's family was much better off than us financially. For a start, my uncle had been left some money and he bought two old houses; the family lived in the one while the other was let to his eldest daughter and her husband. The bath for both houses was in the kitchen of my aunt's home: it had a lid that came down and was used as a seat when the bath wasn't in use.

My cousin and I had some really good fights. We would really get stuck into each other and roll on the ground, still fighting. My one dread was that my cousin would attain better marks than me, and that she would tell the "Aunts." My pride was the only thing I had which was mine alone, and which was most important to me. We seemed, though, to attain the same level in most subjects. We didn't have school uniforms and I was very glad that I was bigger than my cousin, which meant I didn't have to wear her cast-off clothes. It would have been sheer agony for me to wear her clothes—that dubious honour was reserved for Margaret. My sister couldn't wear my cast-off clothes because they were already second or third hand when I received them, and already well past their best.

The only thing I remember learning at that school was digging "for Victory" and growing vegetables. There was a lot of propaganda from the government at that time and everyone was urged to grow vegetables as a duty for each family.

I used to walk to the town's library from school, which was about a mile away, and then walk home, which was another two miles. I went most days because at that time we were only allowed the one book. The children's section of the library wasn't very well stocked and I soon got through all the books there. I decided to start on the adult section. The problem, however, was that children were not allowed in that part of the library. I got around that by saying I was getting a book for my mom. I never had any guidance or encouragement at all on what to read, and read mountains of books before I finally found whatever it was I was looking for. There was only the one lady assistant and she was unmarried. In those days when a professional lady got married she usually had to give up her job, which was a great shame because it left only the old maids. The lady in the library worked very hard. Everything had to be written by hand and she had to do the incoming and outgoings; she always seemed to be rushing from one side of the counter to the other. As for the librarian—he didn't seem to do any work at all! He just sat in his office looking over his glasses, peeping through the window. There were big notices all around the place saying, "SILENCE."

I was still doing different things to earn some pocket money running errands, taking the neighbours' bets, and baby minding. I had saved a small amount of money when the school began to give music lessons. For some unknown reason I decided I would like to learn to play the violin. The violin cost twenty-five shillings (one pound and twenty-five pence) which we could pay off at the rate of a shilling a week. The lessons also cost a shilling a week, and mom agreed to pay the shilling for the violin while I managed to earn the shilling for my lessons. I carried on with the lessons for several weeks, but, no matter how hard I tried, I didn't seem to make much progress. It certainly didn't help having to listen to my family's unprintable comments about my practising. I was finally delegated to the bedroom that was the farthest away from the living room. Unfortunately for me, all my family were music lovers. I was too, but I really did try, if only to prove my family wrong and that I could do it; but the only tune I ever mastered was *The Bells of St Mary*—and that was only on a very good day.

Once, while I was practising, the clock stopped for good. This, for some unknown reason, was blamed on my playing! On another occasion the dog howled to be let out. He ran like the clappers and we didn't see him again for a whole week! Clearly he couldn't stand the noise any more than my family. (Could it be that we had a music-loving dog!) After a time I got the message and decided I couldn't play the violin, or any other instrument; I couldn't sing either, so I decided the very best way for me to enjoy music in future was to listen to people with talent who were much more prepared to dedicate their time and efforts to their music than I was. I took the violin back to school and the Headmistress promised to sell it to another child, and to give me back all the shillings my mom had paid when she had all of the twenty-five shillings. It must have taken her an awfully long time to re-sell that violin, for I'm still waiting for the money. (That could be my fault, of course; after all, I've since changed my name and moved house six times, so I might have been difficult to track!)

After all the years of hospital visits my eyesight hadn't improved and it was decided that when I was fourteen I should have an operation for my "idle eye." After the operation both of my eyes had to be bandaged for a fortnight and throughout that time I had to lie as still as possible. When the bandages finally came off I remember, to my disgust and shame, that my hair was full of head lice! After all that trouble the operation wasn't successful, either, and I now had double vision—*and* still had my "Idle eye." (Or, as the children so cruelly called me when I was younger, I was still "Cock-eyed.")

By this time my dad had become very ill. My younger brother had joined the navy and dad wanted his family around him. He couldn't understand why he couldn't see both of his sons. He called for them all the time. It was a terrible hard time for my mom, trying to help and pacify him, and at the same time worrying about both my brothers.

By now my elder brother Eric was in Europe and my other brother Bernard was in the Far East. Their letters didn't reach us very often and when they did they had been censored. We used to listen to "Lord Haw Haw"—the German propagandist—when we tuned the wireless to the German wavelength. He would announce just where the Germans were going to bomb next. He seemed to know the layout of the Black Country very well and it was quite scary when he mentioned each town by name and said "Germany had the can openers to open our cans" (shelters). He was very intimidating, but we listened to him nevertheless. He always started his programme with the words, "Germany calling, Germany calling!" On one occasion he mentioned the name of the ship my brother was serving on, saying it had had a direct hit and there were no survivors. My mom was sick with worry. She didn't know just what to do. That, I think, was her very lowest time—letters from my brothers weren't getting through, my dad was dying and repeatedly calling for his sons, while my brothers were in fact thousands of miles from each other, neither of them knowing just how ill dad was. Mom had to give up her evening job to look after dad, which meant my sister was the only one bringing money into the home. With all the worry of dad's illness and the terrible anxiety about the safety of both of my brothers, plus the never-ending financial struggle, it must have been the very worst of all of mom's hard times. It was many months before we heard officially that the ship hadn't sunk, though it had been badly damaged with a large hole in its side. It had managed to limp into some port. My brother was safe, although the gun flash had damaged his eyes. He was sent to a hospital in America where he spent his nineteenth birthday. He was made a great fuss of and had lots of presents and a cake made for him there, and had the benefit of lots of visitors.

I was just fourteen when my dad died at home. I remember my maiden aunt was with us a lot of the time. She was a nurse. I think she helped mom a great deal. I remember that she went into dad's bedroom with me and held my hand while he lay dying. I still can't even begin to describe my feelings of terrible unhappiness at fourteen while standing by that bed and watching my dad die. Mostly, I felt an awful sense of bewilderment and most certainly guilt. My dad was fifty when I was born and most of my life he had been ill. He was eagerly awaiting his sixty-fifth birthday when he would receive his pension and a bit more money would be coming into the home. He died at home on Eric's twenty-third birthday and just three weeks before his own birthday. I remember that mom had played quiet games with us to keep us quiet when we were small and he was ill. Like the rest of us, he adored mom. But she was the one who had done everything for us. She had made a safe world for us in all of our troubled times. She was the centre of my universe.

I felt an awful sense of guilt because I wasn't nearly as close to dad as I was to my mom, and I always knew I didn't have the same great love for him I had for my mom. It might be truer to say that I did love him but hadn't told him so. I made a vow that day that in future I would always tell my family I loved them. (My four lovely grandchildren can vouch that I've religiously kept that vow!)

My aunt took us shopping for our mourning clothes. We were all rigged out in new coats, dresses, shoes and hats—all of which were black. It was the first time in my life I had brand new clothes. I believe that my aunt paid for all our clothes. It was months before either of my brothers heard of dad's death, and then we heard from them both on the same day. My dad used to have his horse racing bets on the strap, and after he died mom sent me to see the bookie and to ask how much money dad owed. She told me the slate was clean, although we both knew it wasn't.

Now that I was fourteen I well knew that I had to leave school and get a job. The bookie offered me a job as a bookies runner, though she could only offer me ten shillings a week in wages. I didn't want that because my great ambition was to get a job in an accountant's office—one where rows of figures would be placed in front of me and all I would have to do all day would be to reckon up the figures. Ever since I was little I had always loved to reckon up!

Another of my cousins had told me there was a job going in the office where she worked and that she would ask for the job for me. I had an interview and was thrilled to be told I had passed the test with flying colours and could have the job of office junior. I was again told the pay was ten shillings a week, and that I would have to go to night school twice a week. I would also have to pay for all the books I would need, and the bus fares. Although I was only fourteen I had a very old head on my shoulders and well knew that was out of the question. The school never gave any advice or help in finding a job.

My sister was the only breadwinner in the family and I knew I had to earn more than ten shillings a week to help ease our financial situation. I was heartbroken—having to lose the job of my dreams even before I had the chance to make a go of it. I was so very bitterly disappointed. But I well knew there was no way I could beat the system. Working-class people were meant to stay working class and to remain at the bottom of the pile—unless of course their country needed them to fight and die. *That* was a completely different matter. I felt very bitter and hurt. It was a terrible disappointment to me. I tried very hard not to let my mom know just how I felt. And so I became a very old and desolate fourteen-year-old.

Nevertheless, my sister got me a job where I could earn more money. On the Friday I left school and on the following Monday I joined the masses and became factory fodder.

13

My sister led me into the factory. It was a very large place and I was completely terrified. As far as I could see there were rows and rows of different machines, all making the same terrible row, the leather belts whizzing round and round. The smell was vile.

I knew instantly I would hate that place. I must have been so terribly scared that I walked down that aisle of machines with my mouth wide open. My sister gave me a nudge and told me to close my mouth because she didn't want her friends to think her sister was a half-wit. How much simpler and easier it would have been for me if I had been a half-wit! I was shown to a very large tapping machine. A girl was with me for the first hour to show me how to do the job. I was shaking with fear, but after she had shown me how the machine worked she left me to get on with it.

My utter terror I remember still!

The machine tapped six nuts in a row. The idea was to rush up and down the machine to try to keep all the six taps working at the same time. It was exhausting work. Before I could get all six taps working the first tap would pass through the nut and it would drop into an ice-cold tank of slurry. (Slurry is some kind of oil, white like milk, but with an evil smell. Its use was to cool the taps.) I had to reach down into the slurry to retrieve the taps. At the bottom of the tank there would be the swarf. (Swarf is bits of the metal from the inside of the nuts.) The slurry would be half way up to my elbow, and often my hand would come out of the tank bleeding with bits of the swarf sticking into my fingers. The taps had to be connected up while the machine was still running. That was a very hard and dangerous thing to do. If I didn't move my hand quickly enough, it would be cut. It was a vile job! The very worst part about it was when the taps cracked and burst. There would be a terribly loud noise; the metal would fly everywhere, often hitting me in the face. Luckily for me I wore glasses that shielded my eyes and gave me some small protection. There was no protective clothing or goggles or any earplugs. When the taps burst I had to go and tell the foreman, who wouldn't be very pleased because that meant he would have to make more taps. He made the taps from a very long machine, which cut the metal and shaped the taps. When the taps broke it meant more work for him, which he definitely wasn't happy about. He would shout at me as if it were my fault the taps had broken! I got scared of going to tell him. It was a lousy, dirty and dangerous job. (Fortunately today, no one, but *no one*, least of all a scared, timid square-peg-in-a-round-hole fourteen year old, has to work on those horrid jobs.)

I was 'piecework,' which meant a timekeeper would stand by me with his watch and time just how long it would take to tap the nuts. Somehow, in his great wisdom, he came to the conclusion that I should have the princely sum of two and a half old pence for tapping a gross of nuts. I worked from eight in the morning until six at night, with an hour for lunch. I went home during the lunch hour. There where no canteens. It was compulsory to work Saturday mornings for everyone over the age of sixteen. I didn't have to work Saturday mornings because I was only fourteen and worked forty-five hours while others worked fifty hours.

I remember the labourer Old Tom. He, like me, was just a number in that factory workforce. The tragedy was, though, that old Tom had been just a number all of his life. He didn't talk much, but I got the impression he had been a soldier in the First World War. When I met him he was in his middle sixties, not too tall, but with a very straight back. He always marched along as if he were still on parade. He had a very proud bearing in spite of being not overly bright. He was definitely one of life's have-nots. Old Tom knew I had just left school and that there was no training for the job, no gradual easing into the workplace. He must have sensed my terror, for although he said nothing, he hovered close at hand. Although there was a difference of fifty years in our ages, I felt Old Tom was an ally. He had never married. He didn't chat up the girls. In fact, he didn't chat much to anyone—he just got on quietly with his labouring. In those days, when someone got too old to work a machine at piecework rates but were too young to retire, they were demoted with loss of pay to labouring jobs—sweeping floors, attending to the brazier fires which were scattered around the factory floor, fetching and carrying for pieceworkers, and being a general dogsbody for everyone. First thing each morning, Old Tom would take off his boots, put on his working shoes, and then polish the boots until he could see his face in them. He would put a pile of rags in each boot and then wrap both boots into another rag. He would then place the rag-wrapped boots into his trolley that he pushed around all day. The trolley contained his brush, shovel and the pile of rags he brought to us to clean our machines and wipe our hands on. We weren't supposed to waste time on washing our hands at work. Every time Old Tom brought some rags to me he would say the same thing: "Every little helps says the woman who pee'd in the sea!"

Poor Old Tom! He left a big impression in my scared mind. Much later I did manage to escape, but all of his life Old Tom never stood the least chance of escaping. I could never understand why, but my sister liked her job and seemed quite content working in that horrid place. She had lots of friends there and they would sing while working. A Nelson Eddy and Jeanette Macdonald film was showing at the local cinema, and my sister and her friends would belt out *The Indian Love Call* at the top of their voices. The refrain "When I'm calling You—Hoo—Hoo" had to be belted out with great gusto and very loudly to be heard above the fearful clatter of those machines!

After getting used to the machine I found a marvellous way to counteract the boredom.

I would count down the many minutes, then seconds I had to work until break time, then lunch time, then finally until finishing work for the day. I have always been a compulsive counter and would be adding, dividing, subtracting all day. It helped me to get through the day. It made life and that horrid job more bearable. I was doing the job of tapping the nuts, being frozen all day with my hands continually in the freezing slurry, fingers bleeding, earning the magnificent sum of two and a half pence per gross of nuts tapped.

But I wasn't part of that machine with an off and on button. Although my hands were doing the job they were required to do, my mind was elsewhere. I was quite sure my brains were worth much more. So I didn't intend to waste them on such a futile job. My first week's wages, which I had worked forty-five hours for, amounted to the princely sum of eighteen shillings (90 pence)! The office didn't keep any record of just how much money we had earned. In my case they didn't have to, for I had already worked out my colossal sum.

Friday evening after we had finished work we had to stand in a long queue for our wages. Two women would be sitting at a table. On the table were hundreds of little tins with a number on each one. We had to tell the women our works number and we would be handed our own tin with our wages inside. There was no pay slip or any account of deductions—just money inside the tins. We had to move along the line, then put the empty tins onto another table. I never let on to my mom just how much I hated that job. She had more than enough to worry about with both my brothers serving in the forces, and my dad having just died, without me adding to her troubles.

I remember that I rushed home that first payday, all eighteen shillings of my hard-earned wages tightly clasped in my hands. The look of great relief on my mom's face almost—*though not quite*—made up for that horrid job.

I had four shillings pocket money from my wages. We had a ten-minute break during the morning and weren't allowed to stop work a second before the buzzer sounded. This meant we didn't have time to wash our hands. When the screeching noise started I would dry my hands on a piece of rag Old Tom had given me. I would find an empty box that I would turn upside down to sit on, get out my flask of tea and my sandwiches, then eat my sandwiches, making sure the newspaper they were wrapped in was between my fingers and the food! I much preferred the print from the newspaper to the taste of the slurry on my fingers. Exactly ten minutes later the buzzer would sound again—this time to resume work. If I hadn't drunk my tea or eaten my sandwiches in that time, it was just too bad. We had to start back to work immediately. The manager would walk up and down the aisles to make sure everyone was back on their machines. I'm sure he must have been standing there just waiting for the sound of the buzzer!

Once, while working, I heard a terrible scream. Everyone was running about, screaming and panicking. A young girl had her hair caught in the belt of the machine. The machine couldn't be turned off in time and she was scalped! The manager was running about like a scalded cat. I expect the works would get into some serious trouble. Everyone was terribly upset. I remember that I was absolutely petrified of going back onto my own machine. After that we were all issued with caps with a snood around the side to keep our hair in place.

There was a lady supervisor, but I thought she must have been more like a warden. She was big, frightening and intimidating. She certainly scared the life out of me! Her office was directly opposite the women's toilet and she would sit there all day, timing everyone going in and out of the toilet.

It wasn't quite against the rules to go to the toilet, but it was frowned on if we went in the work's time. There was a row of six toilets, but if two friends tried to enter the toilets at the same time, the supervisor would send one of them back to wait until the other had come out. She would suspect them of wanting to waste time talking about boyfriends, or worse still they may have wanted to have a quick smoke. She used to time everyone going into the toilets, and if they were there longer than she thought they should be, she would walk up and down the row banging on the doors and looking for the telltale sign of smoke. If anyone were caught more than once she would report them to the management and they would get the sack. That was a woman who certainly relished her work!

I worked close to double doors that had to be kept open most of the day for goods coming in and out of the factory. The wind, rain, and snow used to blow in on me while I worked. I was always cold and I suffered from very painful chilblains on both of my ankles (which I treated by rubbing half an onion onto the chilblains). My right hand, which seemed to spend most of the day in icy slurry, became wrinkled and looked horrible. I had a lot of time off with bad colds, and once was away quite a while with pneumonia. Needless to say I didn't receive any sick pay.

We had one week's holiday a year without pay. We were told, however, that although the machines would be turned off that week, we could go into work and clean all the machines and the floors. My sister and I both volunteered to do those jobs. It was very eerie in the factory without the noise of the machines, and without many of the work-force. We were given shovels and had to start at the top of the aisles and work down, scraping the year's grime off the floors. We also had to clean out the slurry tanks and empty out all the dirty slurry and the swalf. It was a filthy job, even filthier than my usual job. I believe I had about two pounds wage that week. My sister would have received more than me because she was older.

Although I really hated that job I managed to stick it out for nearly two years! Finally I left just before my sixteenth birthday. If I had waited until my birthday I wouldn't have been allowed to leave. Although it was almost the end of the war, there were still restrictions on anyone over the age of sixteen changing their jobs—so I suppose there was some very small consolation for me in being younger. During my working life I've worked in dozens of factories, but never again was I so scared, so defenceless, as in that first vile job. I was so terribly unhappy and frightened, having been thrown into the deep end at the very tender age of fourteen.

14

Now that I was working and bringing money into the home, I was an adult in the eyes of the Black County scenario. That meant the jobs I had had to do around the house would be passed down to the next youngest, which had happened to me when my brother had left school. It also meant now I could read in peace without being told to get my nose out of a book and do some housework! I was rich with my four shillings pocket money, so my friend and I would go to the pictures twice a week. The trouble, though, was that she had to take along her ten-year-old brother and he was a right little pain! We always bought ten woodbines between us. We had four each and we had to give the other two to her brother to bribe him so he wouldn't report back to their mother that my friend had been smoking. All three of us would be spluttering and choking, but we were determined to enjoy those cigarettes! We usually went Monday night, and again on the Thursday when there would be a different film showing. I remember that on both those nights there would be three old men attending the pictures. They would call for one another. It didn't matter to them just what kind of film was showing—they still went to the same cinema and sat in the same seats. One of them would take an old tin can with him and they would kick the can all the way from their homes to the cinema. They would shove and push each other, just like the big kids they really were. The can would go into the road and they would chase after it. Luckily there wasn't much traffic about in those days. The traffic there was always managed to drive around them. The drivers would shout out a few choice words that didn't bother those old men who came out with quite rude gestures and a few choice words of their own. When they reached the cinema the can would be carefully placed behind the entrance door so that no one could see or move it; then, when they came out of the cinema, they would retrieve it and begin the whole process again on the way home. It was weird, really weird, but they were quite harmless. Watching the TV programme *Last of the Summer Wine*, I was reminded of those old men of long ago.

There was also a very fat lady who went to the same cinema twice a week. She was *really* huge—so much so that she couldn't sit in just the one seat: she always sat in a double seat, several of which were placed around for courting couples. No one else was ever allowed to sit in the double seat she favoured, even if she wasn't there—just in case she decided to turn up. She had a loud voice to match the rest of her body. People moved out of her way pretty sharpish. The local people knew which was her seat and kept well clear; but if anyone were silly enough to sit in 'her' seat she would have physically removed them out by their ears.

We tried to get to the cinema long before the last house started so that we could see the beautiful organ rising up through the floor. It was a magnificent sight! The sound would swell, louder and louder, then the organist's head, then body would appear. The whole thing fascinated me. The organist, who was also the manager and had a house next door to the cinema, could make that organ talk. He would play all the popular tunes of the day and everyone sang at the top of their voices. It was a magical atmosphere for just those few minutes.

There was always lots of war news, and a great deal of propaganda. Then there would be a small film or cartoon, then finally the big film. Usually it was a sloppy Hollywood love story. I believe that was deliberate to boost the morale of the people. For a couple of hours the cinema allowed us to sit in reasonable comfort and forget the war and our jobs. It was our only escape route from the terrible harsh world of reality, an escape everyone took advantage of, for the cinemas were always packed out. I always sat back and imagined it was me in the arms of Clark Gable, James Steward, Spencer Tracy and all the other great stars of the time. In between each film the lights would go on and the usherette would come along and spray some kind of scent all over the place.

It was quite a powerful aroma and if it were sprayed too near us it would catch our breath. She also went down the rows telling people to leave if they had already seen the films, because there were always people standing at the back waiting for their seats. There would be very long queues outside; when half a dozen people went out, only half a dozen more were allowed in. When we saw the usherette bearing down on us we would make a dive for the toilets and try to gauge just how long it would take her to go down the rows; then, when we thought the coast was clear, we would double back to our seats.

We could only afford to be in the 'Spitters'—the cheapest seats—which cost us ten old pence; but sometimes we would be really cheeky and instead of going back to our cheap seats we would make a dive for the 'One and Nines'—the dearer seats. Often the usherette would cotton on to our tricks and ask to see our tickets. We would rush out of the cinema a few seconds before the end of the film so we wouldn't have to stand to attention while the national anthem was played. Everyone else seemed to have the same idea, for there would be a mad scramble and people would be almost falling over to get out!

The fat lady lived in the street that backed onto ours. Her back garden joined on to our neighbour's garden, and although we could see our own house just a few feet away we had to walk round three streets to get to our home. So, when we came out of the pictures feeling tired and weary, we were looking for a short cut, and going through her garden saved us a lot of time and shoe leather. Sometimes, though, the fat lady would be sitting at her front window, just watching the world go by. We well knew there was no way she would give us permission to go down her garden path and climb over the fence into our neighbour's garden. But we were too tired to care, so almost taking our lives in our hands we would try to avoid eye contact with her, then lift up the latch on her front gate and run like the clappers through her front garden; we would get to the really scary place (her back door), then dash down the back garden to climb over the fence to safety. She would amble out of her back door with a rolling pin, thankfully just a few seconds after we had managed to run past. She would wave the rolling pin and shout at us, "I'll get you one of these days, you cheeky young buggers!" She never did catch us, though. We always knew we were fairly safe—she was much too fat to run. I don't know if she would actually have hit us with the rolling pin if ever she caught us! Perhaps she was just playing a game with us. Luckily we could run faster than she could, so we were never in the unfortunate position of finding out.

I remember 'D' Day—the 6th of June 1940, very well. It was my sister-in-law's twenty-first birthday, and it was a really terrible day. She and mom spent the whole day crying. They both realised my brother would be in the thick of the fighting. Eric and his wife had a five-week-old baby boy, my brother had never seen his son, and it was a very long while after the war was over before he did see the baby. My sister-in-law had to live with us because there was a great shortage of houses. When working-class young couples got married there was no chance whatsoever of them having their own homes. At the age of fourteen they could work on highly dangerous and unsafe machines. At the age of eighteen they could go to war—they could even kill and be killed for their country. But they weren't allowed to vote until they were twenty-one; nor could they expect to want or have their own homes. Young married couples had to live with their mother-in-laws. I don't think it was too bad if it were the young man living with his in-laws; but it must have been very hard for young wives when their husbands came on leave and they were living at his mother's home; then she would have to share his precious time with his family, and they wouldn't have any privacy at all. It was especially hard for them living with in-laws if there was friction when their husbands were away at the war. Fortunately for us we all got on well together.

It was unheard of for people in our circumstances to buy, or indeed to have the opportunity to buy their own homes. In some homes there would be three, or even four women in the one kitchen. That certainly didn't make for harmony.

Now that I was fourteen and with childhood behind me I was classed as adult, so there were now four women in our household. Mom did all the shopping and cooking, so our kitchen wasn't a total war zone; nevertheless, we had more than our share of bad moments. My sister-in-law had her baby at home. It was very rare for anyone to have their confinement in hospital, unless there was the possibility of complications. The midwife was the only single lady I knew who was allowed a council house. I believe it was a perk of her job. She lived in the next street to us. I often went with my sister-in-law when she had to go for antenatal visits to the midwife's house. I don't know why I went with her—maybe it was because I was nosy and hated to miss anything. Once the labour pains started I was the one who raced for the midwife. I stood watching my mom boiling the water and gathering up lots of towels. I sat on the stairs listening to all the commotion. There seemed to be a considerable amount of activity going on. I listened to my sister-in-law's cries of pain. I heard her vainly calling my brother's name over and over. I was very fond of her and her pain disturbed me so much that I decided there and then I would never have any babies! When I heard the cry of the baby, though, it was the most beautiful sound I had ever heard! I was soon allowed into the bedroom to see my gorgeous nephew who had the red hair of our family. I loved him at first sight!

I decided that having babies was perhaps not so dreadful after all.

My fourteenth year was quite eventful. I had been with my dad when he died. I had started work doing a job I hated, and I had become an aunt. I had certainly put my childhood firmly behind me. I spent many hours minding my little nephew, and I loved to show him off. Often I would read to him, to try to get him to sleep; sometimes I even sang a lullaby to him though my singing was no better than my violin playing. I think some of the time he pretended to be asleep just to shut me up! He was a very smart little baby. Some of the time I was so tired I fell asleep before he did.

I read in the evening paper that young girls could apply to have farming working holidays. I thought that sounded great as I had never been on holiday in my life. I persuaded Jessie and two of her friends to come with me. They said they would if I did all the arranging. I sent off for all the information, only to find that at fourteen years of age I was considered too young! I was bitterly disappointed but still made all the arrangements for the others. I helped to carry their cases to the railway station. They had all bought slacks and thought they looked great, though there were two women chatting over their garden gate as we went by and they shouted at the girls, asking them why they wanted to dress like boys! They all had a fabulous holiday and came back very brown from working all day on the farms.

15

A part from the mourning clothes my aunt had bought for me and which we had to wear for the twelve-month mourning period following my dad's death, I had never had any brand new clothes. Now, though, things seemed to be getting easier in our household. Now that the twelve months of mourning had passed, mom bought yards and yards of beautiful dark blue material and a young girl in our street made dresses for my two sisters and I. We had to go to her house to be measured, though I hated to go there because her sixteen-year-old brother was always in the room. I was embarrassed at his being there, but he always stayed put. All three of us had the same pattern and style—a long plain bodice with buttons down the back and a pleated skirt. I don't know just why we had the same design, but I do know we all thought we were the cat's whiskers. Our ages were twelve, fifteen and twenty-one. I doubt that sisters with such a wide age spread would be happy with that arrangement today.

Mom decided we could now afford our very first holiday. There was great excitement and happiness just at the thought of going to the seaside! I started a 'diddleum club' between us. (That's a saving club where the payments go up each week.) I think I started the club with us all paying a shilling and then going up an extra penny each week, until we reached the vast amount of two shillings. That was half of my pocket money, so I think that when we reached that large amount I would have stopped there. I always loved counting and adding up. I kept all of the money in a drawer in the bedroom and had great pleasure in counting it over and over again, even though only a very small portion of the money was mine. My family were quite happy with my handling of their money.

My favourite aunt had been on that holiday before and she did all the arranging because she knew all the details. She sent off ten shillings deposit for each of the two chalets booked. We began to count off the months, then the weeks, then the days. My aunt never counted the time in months; she would say, "It's only six more fortnights to our holiday!" She said the time went quicker that way.

Food was still rationed, so mom tried to save items of grocery from our rations each week. We had to take the whole week's food rations with us. Mom kept sugar in empty tins that had originally held the baby's dried milk. At that time even babies' food was rationed, being so many points a tin. Mom saved those tins, just as she saved everything else, knowing that at some time there would be a use for them. She put a layer of sugar, then an egg, then another layer of sugar, then another egg, then sugar again and so on, until the tin was full. We carried those tins for a hundred miles and I don't believe we had one cracked egg!

The great day finally arrived—we were going on holiday! It was hard work carrying the cases. We had borrowed shopping bags and all manner of containers that had to hold enough clothes and food for the week for all four of us. We all had our quota to carry. We were on our way, making sure all the neighbours knew well in advance we were going on holiday. We had a short bus ride, lugging our belongings on and off the busses with great difficulty. We met up with my aunt and her three children—a girl and boy, twins my age, and a boy a year younger. Then we had to walk to the coach station, stopping every few minutes to change the luggage from one hand to the other. Fortunately we had allowed ourselves plenty of time to spare before the coach departed.

It was a great relief to hand over the cases to the driver, although we still held on to the bags that contained the sandwiches and bottles of lemonade for the journey. The driver got into his seat, released the handbrake, and we were away at long last! I was finally going to the sea-side—my first holiday ever at the advanced age of fifteen! Soon I would be seeing the sea for the first time in my life.

Great happiness exuded from all of us. We laughed and sang every inch of the way. I'm quite sure no one ever looked forward to a holiday more than we did that marvellous time. The war was finally over, life was still very hard for us all, but at least the pressure was off. There would be no more bombings and killings. Both of my brothers had come through the war safely. We could relax, knowing we would soon see them again. Mom could now sleep at nights, knowing her sons would be home one day. We could begin to live for ourselves—at last! We had had our share of the blood, sweat and tears. Now we were going to enjoy ourselves: we were determined to be happy, come what may.

After a long tiring journey we finally arrived at the seaside. I had long been looking through the window, hoping to catch my very first glance of the sea, and was disappointed to find the tide was out. The driver dropped us off at Rhyl and sorted out our cases. But we were still quite a way from the camp. By this time we were weary and longing for a cup of tea, but still had to endure another tiring bus ride before reaching our destination. Again we had to push and shove our cases on and off a bus, until we finally reached the camp. Alighting from the bus, we were surprised and pleased to see dozens of small boys with homemade trolleys, wheelbarrows, old prams and all sorts of home-made contraptions on four wheels. They were pushing and shoving each other for custom, being very enterprising—future entrepreneurs, who knows? Some of those lads may well be millionaires by now, though certainly not by virtue of the sixpenny tip we collected between us to give them to cart our luggage the last few yards. We had to report to the site office where a lady took all our particulars. She gave us two keys and told us where our huts were. We made our way with the luggage boys still tagging along earning their sixpenny tip.

Our huts were next to each other. It was an old army camp and the huts were old—very old and dilapidated billets. (I doubt if people would be allowed to keep animals in a place like that today.) The inside of the huts had been partitioned into three rooms. Two of the rooms held a double bed and a locker—that was all. There was no place to keep our clothes. The other bigger room was a kitchen cum sitting room. We were all busy, trying to find a space for everything, which certainly wasn't easy. There were very few cupboards. Having the week's rations for four of us meant there were quite a lot of tin food, meat, biscuits and cakes which mom had baked. By this time we were all gasping for a cup of tea, but it wasn't yet to be. We had to wait while a man came and fixed the calor gas for us and then pay him for the week's supply of the gas. There was no water in the chalet, so our next job was to search for a water container; then we had to find the cold water tap which was a good two hundred yards away.

When we did finally locate the tap, it was only to find that other people had the same idea, for there was a great long queue. Our high spirits still carried us along, although by this time we were all weary. When we finally got that cup of tea it must have been the best cuppa ever! Looking back now, the amount of work, the time and effort we all put into that first holiday seems incredible, yet at the time we all thought it was well worth the trouble. The toilets, fortunately for us, or unfortunately if we were in a hurry, were quite a long way from our chalet. They were just buckets with lids on the top. Needless to say the smell was indescribable, especially towards the end of the day when they were over full. The doors were just a thin piece of wood, which swung backwards and forwards. There were no locks or any fasteners at all. My sisters and I used to go together so that we could keep guard for one another. A man emptied the buckets early afternoon, and again at night. He would take the over-full buckets away, and then put clean ones in their place. We would watch out for his coming and going; when he had finished we would make a dive there before the clean buckets had a chance to fill up again. He dug a hole to bury the refuse.

Behind the so-called toilets was a pigsty, and it was quite scary to hear several fat pigs grunting and groaning. It seemed to me they were only a few yards away from us. We lived in a highly industrial town and knew nothing at all, or for that matter didn't want to know anything, about pigs. I know I was terrified in case the pigs escaped and somehow got into the toilets! I don't know if the pigs were placed next to the toilets to hide that smell, or if it was the other way round and the toilets were placed there to hide the smell of the pigs! Either way it certainly wasn't a place in which to linger.

There was no entertainment at all—no shops on the camp, no wakey wakey. There were just those old army huts, but at least it was the seaside. Our first holiday ever, we thought it was wonderful! Running down to the pebble beach and seeing and smelling the sea for the first time was marvellous.

I had been very daring and had bought my very first brand new pair of slacks, which I rolled up just about showing my knees. (Well, it *was* the seaside, after all.) We carefully dipped our toes into the sea and soon became more adventurous, splashing each other. Venturing into the sea, feeling the cold waves and the sand between my toes was magic to me. Although there wasn't a great deal of space with all eight of us, we were in and out of each other's huts the whole time, laughing, giggling, and playing tricks on one another and having great fun. Mom and my aunt both made mountains of sandwiches which we carried down to the beach to last us all day; then, tired and pleasantly weary, we would make our way back to one of the huts and a cooked tea would be prepared. We all had our different jobs to do to help with the meal, either peeling potatoes, shelling peas, queuing for water, washing up or carrying the shopping. Everyone, including the two boys, had jobs to do, and no one ever moaned. We all did our jobs with a great deal of fun and laughter.

Sometimes, if we had enough money to spare, we would go mad and buy fish and chips to take back to the hut with us. We ate them straight out of the paper to save washing up, for after our frugal experience we were all quite expert at saving money, time and effort. There wasn't enough room for us all to sit down in the one hut, so we removed the partitions and brought the beds forward and so we sat on the beds to eat our meals.

One day we were sitting on a bed larking around, pushing and shoving each other, when *bang!* —the bed collapsed under our combined weight. We all fell down in all directions. It was hilarious, watching mom and my aunt trying to mend that bed, tears of laughter pouring down their cheeks! *Happy, happy days!* I think that holiday was the most looked forward to, the most exciting, and certainly one of the happiest holidays ever.

The price of that holiday was three pounds a week for each hut. On the very last day mom and my aunt each paid a ten-shilling deposit (fifty pence) to secure those same huts for the following year. We were all quieter on the way home, although going back was much easier and lighter, for we no longer had all that food to carry. We were now in a position to brag to everyone who would listen that we had been to the seaside; and more importantly, we were going again the next year!

We were now amongst the elite—the people who went on holidays!

No longer would we have to stand back and *watch* other people going on holidays. We had now been to the seaside ourselves, and much more importantly we were going *again* the next year. We had something to look forward to in the long hard months ahead.

We had finally made it. After many years of struggle, we had finally arrived.

16

It was great when my brothers finally came on leave, although they were never lucky enough to be on leave at the same time. It was a great pleasure, and a marvellous feeling of relief, especially for mom to know they were both safe and sound. Both of my brothers had altered a great deal. Neither of them ever wanted to talk about their war experiences. They had both grown in maturity and adulthood: they had seen many horrors of war.

My sister had become friends again with her boyfriend, Little Sir Echo. He was called up and joined the army, and she wrote to him for all the four years he served. Tragically, just two weeks before the war ended, he was blown up by a mine. She received a letter from the padre, along with a parcel of all the letters she had written to him. He was just twenty-two. The poor lad had never had any life at all.

All of our family were terribly upset. I had had a crush on him since I was nine years old. I remembered him as being a very good-looking lad with bright red hair. My sister kept all of his letters for the rest of her life.

Both of my brothers liked to have a drink. (A small understatement—they went on some right benders!) Once, while on leave, Bernard went out on the tiles with his friend who was on leave from the R.A.F. It was very late and we were all anxiously waiting up for him. Mom was very worried. I don't think any of us quite realised he had been through a war and he wasn't now the young boy who had never been away from home before. Everyone had a great deal of adjusting to do. Anyway, we all sat about waiting for him when suddenly we heard a *clomp, clomp* coming up the street. We heard my brother shouting, "Come in and have some supper with me!" The noise had awakened the whole street. Lights went on in all the bedrooms. The whole place was illuminated! Some of the neighbours came out into the street to see what all the commotion was about. Suddenly our door opened and Bernard came in—leading a horse!

It was pandemonium!

The horse was led around the table. Chairs and everything in its way were sent flying left, right and centre. Everyone except me was chasing about trying to get hold of the rope that the horse had been tethered with. The horse's hooves were flying. The poor beast was bewildered—and so were we! I turned and ran upstairs pretty sharpish, hoping that horses couldn't climb stairs. I had no aspiration of being a heroine—I just wanted to get away from those flying hooves! It was Jessie who finally grabbed hold of the rope and led the horse outside. Bernard was still shouting out that he only wanted to give the horse some supper. The horse ran down the street like the clappers, with Bernard chasing after it and all of us chasing after my brother.

By now the whole street was in an uproar. We never *did* find out just where that horse had come from, or even where it went. There certainly weren't any horses kept in the built-up area we lived in. None of us would have gone within a mile of a horse normally. We had quite a lot of cleaning up to do after that episode. Luckily for us, our visitor didn't leave his calling card.

The same evening Bernard's friend, who was a rear gunner in the R.A.F and had had some scary times, fancied a cheese and pickled onion sandwich when he arrived home. He fetched a full jar of pickled onions from the pantry. The biggest and best onion was right at the bottom of the jar and he tried to spear it, but failed—perhaps because, like my brother, he was ever so slightly intoxicated. He decided it was all too much trouble and the easiest way to resolve the problem was to tip the whole jar upside down. Unfortunately he tipped the onions onto his mom's very best white tablecloth that she'd put out especially in honour of his homecoming.

Another time my brother Bernard went out with our cousin who, for some strange reason, was in a Scottish regiment. I'm quite sure my cousin had never ever been anywhere near Scotland. This lunchtime they were both out drinking in their uniforms, and were enjoying themselves so much that they were holding up the traffic by dancing in the middle of the road. They were doing the hornpipe and a Scottish reel. Bernard wore his naval uniform and a tam'o shanter on his head, while my cousin was in the full dress of his uniform, including the kilt and a sailor's hat. Our neighbour ("Mrs such a thing") saw them dancing and ran home to tell mom. We all quickly ran to rescue them both before they got into any trouble. They both let us bring them home like little lambs. They went to bed to sleep for a couple of hours and were as right as rain for the evening drinking session.

Even though the war was now over it was a long, long time before the men were de-mobbed. My elder brother Eric had been in the army from day one, so he was amongst the first batch of men to be released. For his service to King and Country, he came home in an ill-fitting demob suit and a few pounds gratuity money and no prospects of a good job or any training for one. The promises that had been made of houses fit for heroes on their return from the war were soon forgotten. There weren't any houses for heroes or anyone else. Although my sister-in-law had put their names down for a council house, they had to wait a long while for a house. Meanwhile Eric had to come back to live in the family home, which by now was quite overcrowded. There was a points system for houses: several points for overcrowding, points for how long a couple had been married, extra points if boys and girls had to share rooms. Soon my sister-in-law was again pregnant with a "Demob baby."

This time, though, it was a girl, which brought their points to the top of the list. If she had had another boy she wouldn't have had any extra points. They were allotted a three-bedroom house just after the baby was born. Not before time. Our house was bursting at the seams. It was hard for us all to adjust and for all of us to try to live in harmony. Although we were a very close family, we did have some very bad moments.

Everyone had a great deal of adjusting to do to get to know each other again. It was far from easy. Privacy was impossible to come by in overcrowded homes, and none of us had our own space. Life didn't get any easier for working-class people. It was hard for young men to settle down. They had given years of their lives to fight for their Country, only to find some things were now much worse than before they went away. Jobs were hard to come by and food was still strictly rationed. The services had provided more, and much better food than their civilian rations. Everyone began to wonder just who had won the war. It certainly didn't seem that *we* had.

Like everything else, furniture was very hard to come by. It was on a points system, again. Each couple was allowed only so many. I don't recall just how many points each item was, but one had to think very carefully to get goods in the right order of priority. Most of the furniture was utility. (It was made to last. I still have my aunt's utility cabinet.) Top of the list for my sister-in-law was a bed and cots for the babies, a table and a few chairs. Everything else had to wait.

Even nappies were hard to come by. Mom ripped up very old sheets to make into nappies. She paid a shilling each week for twenty-one weeks into a household shop. (The extra shilling was interest.) There would be a draw, with the numbers one to twenty, and whichever number she drew meant she could have goods to the value of a pound that week. It was fine if she got an early number, which meant she could have the goods almost straight away. The snag, though, was it was a long, long time to carry on paying after receiving the goods. I don't think that shops today would get very far operating that system.

When the week's number mom had chosen came up, I had to go to the shop and choose the biggest washing up bowl the shop had. It was a present for my sister-in-law, to bath the new baby in. It was huge! It was so enormous that the bus conductor wouldn't allow me on the bus with it, and it was a very hard two-mile walk humping that bowl all the way home.

Everyone had gas meters in their homes, which had to be fed with pennies, and the neighbours seemed always to run out of pennies—so we were well used to them knocking on our door at all hours of the day, asking if we had "a penny for two half pennies." After a while it became quite a nuisance, and each time we heard a knock on the door the response would be, "Oh no! Not some neighbour after pennies again!"

My favourite aunt and her husband had taken over a public house and Jessie became their weekend barmaid, and as no one had telephones in those days, the arrangement was if my sister wasn't home by a certain time, we wouldn't wait up for her but would lock up and go to bed.

I was just going off to sleep late one night when I heard someone throwing small pebbles at the window. I sleepily got out of bed, opened the window, looked out, and saw Jessie standing below. I leaned out of the window and asked sleepily, "What do you want?" My very practical sister answered, "A penny for two half pennies! Come down and open the door, you bloody fool!" Margaret and I still had lots of arguments, and sometimes we even fought each other. My jealousy got in the way of us being friends. It wasn't *her* fault that as she got older she became more beautiful! She was small and dainty, whereas I was big, quite plump, in keeping with my nickname 'Pud.' She tried hard to be my friend, but I wasn't having any of that. She always offered to curl or even perm my hair. I always refused, preferring to wear a scarf around my head in the turban fashion. That was silly because, although I didn't have the red hair of my brothers, I did have long, thick chestnut-coloured hair that could have been my crowning glory if only I had given myself half a chance.

I knew it was no use trying to compete with my sister. She had a head start over me, so I didn't even bother. She even offered to lend me her makeup, but I didn't see the point in even trying. I knew people outside of the family compared us—to my disadvantage. I told myself I didn't care. Of course I *did* care—very deeply. My inferiority complex always sat down hard on both of my shoulders. Although my sister was three years younger than me, she had lots of boyfriends knocking on the door. None knocked on the door for me. The aunts would say to me, "Your sister has a boy friend. When are *you* going to get one?" I would tell them I wasn't the least interested in boyfriends, but of course I was.

One Saturday morning, when mom had gone shopping, there was only Margaret and I downstairs. Bernard was home on leave and was still in bed fast asleep. We were doing the housework between us and listening to the wireless at the same time when a jazz band I really hated came on. Although I love music I couldn't stand jazz! I still can't, especially that particular band, so I turned the wireless off. Margaret knew just how much I disliked that band so she turned the wireless on again and she increased the volume. I immediately turned it off again. It went off and on several times; each time it went back on, the volume was increased more. My temper finally boiled right over. All I can remember is everything going black. I lunged for my sister and this time it wasn't the usual argument and thumping match. Instead, my hands were around her neck!

I completely lost all control of myself and was pressing her neck. She was screaming and struggling, but I was much bigger than she was. She had no chance against me. I just don't know what was happening. I don't know if I would have come to my senses in time, but suddenly—thankfully!—I felt hands on the scruff of my neck. I felt myself being pulled away and thrown right across the living room.

All the noise had woken up Bernard who had rushed downstairs to see what all the commotion was. Margaret was screaming at me: "You're mad! You're bloody mad!" I was still lying on the floor, staring at my hands that were shaking and which seemed to have grown, they seemed so huge. I was more scared than I have ever been in my life, before or since. I was certainly more scared even than my sister. I think for a few seconds I had lost my senses. I don't know just what would have happened had Bernard not been on leave.

That episode scared us both so very much that we declared an unspoken truce.

17

By the time I was seventeen I decided I had had enough of factory work for a time. It didn't get a lot easier. Margaret was now fourteen and working, so our family financial situation finally seemed to have eased. It seemed a good time to look for something new.

I would have loved to have an office job. My original ambition was to have some job in accounting, but after three years in factories, and at the grand old age of seventeen, there was no chance whatsoever of me ever attaining my ambition. At fourteen we were slotted into a place and that was it, whether we were suited to the job or not. The people in offices always looked down on factory workers and didn't want to know about anyone who worked or had worked in factories. Although I was a square peg in a round hole and was very good at maths, I realised I would never have my dream job.

One day I saw an advertisement for a junior in a large household store, so I decided to apply. I had to see the manager, who gave me a list with dozens of sums to work out in a certain time. That was no problem for me. I did them in record time and I was delighted when he said the job was mine. The pay was two pounds a week plus monthly commission. There were twelve staff altogether—the manager, his assistant, one warehouse worker, the cashier, one lady who worked part-time to make up the curtains and do any alterations the customers wanted doing, two senior assistants, four juniors, and—to me the most important member of the staff—Jeanie the Scottish cook. For me the very best part of the job was my lunch break when I went upstairs to the staff room and got fussed over by the motherly Jeanie. She would have the table all laid; a beautiful clean white cloth was freshly ironed and changed every day. She fussed around us juniors like a mother hen. She was a superb cook and changed the menu each day. She produced lots of Scottish dishes. We had a three-course meal for a few pence. Jeanie's meals were the only highlight of my day. Being the last one in, I was the *junior* Junior, which meant that when the commission was dished out I was at the bottom of the pile! I was placed in the worst of all departments and put on the haberdashery counter, which meant there was virtually no commission. I never had the least chance of any big orders. I seemed to spend my days selling buttons, which in those days were not on cards but kept all together in a massive box. There were big, little, middle sized, fat, thin, red, blue, green, grey, brown, and white buttons. It was a nightmare, especially if someone wanted a set of half a dozen buttons and I could only find five! It would take ages to find that last elusive button.

Stock taking was the time I really dreaded, for all the buttons, ribbons, belts, buckles, tapes, cotton, needles and pins had to be placed in the right order, then counted. Then everything had to be written down. It was a boring, fiddly job.

We had our own sales book, which was duplicated, and when we made a sale we had to take our books and the customer's money to the cashier, who would then mark the books and give us the change to give back to the customer. The cashier was an old-fashioned spinster, very close to retirement age. She thought all juniors were the lowest of the low. She sat all day locked in her little box of an office, which was only about four feet by six feet wide; the glass was strengthened, with only a small slit to put the books and money through. If we were talking, or having a laugh, she would bend down and shout at us through the little slit. I never remember her smiling, or even having a laugh. She was always stern looking and very soberly dressed. She had her hair in an old-fashioned bun, and it was impossible to imagine she had ever been young, in love, a teenager or a baby! She must have been born old. She always had a permanent headache, poor woman, for her life certainly wasn't a happy one.

Once a week the owner of the store condescended to call. The manager would tell his assistant, and the assistant told the seniors who would in turn tell the juniors, so that everything would be shipshape before the great one arrived.

The owner was a little old man with snow-white hair and a beard, and he looked very much like Grumpy of the seven dwarfs. He would bustle in, look right through us, the juniors, just as if we were invisible. The senior ladies would fawn and open doors for him, and he would sail through without a word of thanks. He then went into the little cubby-hole with the cashier where they would go through the accounts.

That must have been the time she dreaded most of all! She would be bowing and scraping, practically kissing his feet. Then he would march out and she would lock the door after him with a great feeling of relief, safe and sound in the knowledge that her job in her own little glass world was secure for another week at least.

The time I liked best of all was the approach to Christmas when the store had thousands of cheap toys. We worked overtime after the store was closed, packing the toys in pink and blue parcels, and then putting them in different coloured sacks. The store would then employ an old man to play Father Christmas. (The owner would have been ideal for the role of Father Christmas, with his white beard, but he was far too miserable, and he just didn't know how to smile!) There would be queues all through the store and down the street. It was a very busy time. Even the juniors managed to get some sales and a minute commission.

There was a window dresser who came once a fortnight to change the displays. I think he may have been self-employed. He was quite brilliant at his job—a true 'artiste' at work. One time the window would have a blue background, at other times different colours, but always with matching materials draped all around the window. Models were beautifully dressed with matching accessories of hats, scarves, gloves, shoes and handkerchiefs. People out shopping would stop and watch while he worked. Often there would be a crowd gathered, looking at his marvellous display, which was a labour of love to him and was carefully arranged with great attention to detail. If a customer wanted anything from the window we had to check first through the stock, making absolutely sure before anything was ever moved from the display. One day, however, a customer asked me for something from the window. I searched through all the stock but couldn't find the item she wanted. The senior assistant was away at her lunch. I was hoping the customer would settle for something else but she was adamant the article she wanted was the one in the window.

Juniors weren't allowed to climb into the window space, but there was no one else about, the customer was getting impatient with me, and I had been told the customer was always right! So, although I was absolutely terrified, especially as the store was packed out, I knew I had to climb into that window. I very carefully reached for the article, but not nearly carefully enough. I bumped into one of the models, sending it flying; that in turn knocked over another model, then another, until they all came falling down like a pack of cards. There was a crowd outside looking in at the window and they all began to clap! I think they wondered just what I would do for an encore. Although there had been no senior staff about when I needed them, they all magically appeared from all directions to see the devastating mess I had caused!

I was terribly scared and embarrassed. This is it, I thought—the chop for me! I had to report to the manager and I was surprised that he didn't give me the sack. However, he did give me a right telling off, and told me in no circumstances must I *ever* go near the window display again. That was fine by me!

The store was quite a long way from home and the bus fares were taking out a big chunk from my two-pound a week wages; so I decided to buy a second-hand bike that turned out to be a major mistake. I could hardly stay on the bike and hadn't any road sense at all! Luckily there wasn't a great deal of traffic about in those days, which was just as well for me. One day, however, when I was riding down quite a steep road, the brakes gave out on me. There was a young couple walking arm in arm towards me and I went straight through them. I'm quite sure neither of them had ever moved so quickly in their lives! She went one way, he the other. The young man called out a few choice words after me—words I cannot repeat here. I did wonder, though, if his young lady knew he had such a flowery vocabulary. If she hadn't known before, she did then. I may have done her a favour! In any case that was the end of my bicycling and I've never been on a bike since.

After we had our lunch, a couple of juniors and myself would go round the market and the shops. One day we went into a sweet shop I had never been in before. The two girls were being served while I waited at the back of the shop—but although the girls were being served the lady was staring at me the whole time. I became quite uncomfortable and uneasy, having done nothing wrong. I desperately wanted to walk out of the shop, but I thought why should I? I felt guilty of something I hadn't done, and I knew my face was getting redder. The girls, seeing my discomfort, began to snigger, which made me feel even worse. I was determined to stand my ground, nevertheless. Finally, when the girls had been served and we all began to move to go out of the shop, the lady pulled up the flap of the counter, came round the other side, walked up to me and, placing her hand on my shoulder, said, "Excuse me, just a minute, but are you Fanny Blick's daughter?" Surprised, I said yes—that was my mom's maiden name.

It appeared the lady had been in the same class as mom. They had in fact been best friends at school, but had lost sight of each other when they left school at fourteen. It had been over forty years since they had seen each other. It seemed remarkable to me that she had recognised a seventeen-year-old she had never seen before as the daughter of a girl she went to school with all those many years before! When I went home and told mom, she was amazed and the very next day went to the shop to renew her old acquaintance and to have a good old natter about old times. After that episode I never got any peace from my workmates: from that time on I was always called "Fanny Blick's daughter!"

One day, after the "Mighty One, the owner" had made his weekly appearance, another junior and I were called into the manager's office and told that business was bad—the shop had to make redundancies and as we were the last to get jobs there, we had to be the first to go. I just couldn't understand how our two pounds each week could make that much difference to the outcome of the shop. The manager was very sorry and assured us our work was good, and that it was no fault of ours that we had to go—business was simply slack, and he promised us excellent references. (Oddly, we had just worked through a very busy Christmas.) He promised faithfully that when the business picked up he would call us back. The trade at that shop must be really, really slow, for I'm *still* waiting for my re-call! (But again, perhaps the fault is mine: having changed my name once and my address six times, he might have had trouble finding my present whereabouts—although by now I may be more than a bit long in the tooth for the job of junior! I could be the oldest junior in the country. Who knows, I might even make it into the Guinness book of records!) Anyway, I had already got fed up with the job and working all day Saturday, so I wasn't too upset, I suppose—although I would have preferred more notice for job hunting. We weren't allowed any time off to look for another job, or given any extra wages, which meant I was out of pocket until I could find another job. I was jobless for several days, and without money, a position I could ill afford to be in.

18

During the winter of 1947 we had the worst weather for many years with very deep snowdrifts that lasted for weeks. Everyone was snowed in and it seemed to us that the snow would be there forever; but after a while people began to clear the snow, each family clearing the path in front of their own house so the footpath was cleared for people walking down the whole street. The snow was piled very high in the gutters. A neighbour across the road from us struggled to go to work every day. He was quite small and we used to stand at the window to watch out for his coming and going, because all we could see was his cap bobbing up and down over the piled-up snow. It was really funny and my brother made up some good rhymes about him.

During that time mom was taken very ill in the middle of the night. It was a terrible time. My brother battled through the snow to fetch the doctor. He had to walk a long, long way, and then wait to carry the doctor's bag; then they both struggled through the snow and both were exhausted when they arrived back home. The doctor had to examine mom by candlelight, for the electricity had failed.

The coal man couldn't get through to deliver any coal, either. Bernard and I each wheeled a barrow with great difficulty through the drifts to the coal yard, where there was a very long queue. People had all kinds of contraptions on wheels to get the coal home. I seem to remember that we were a very long time in that queue and we were both freezing cold as we watched the huge pile of coal getting smaller and smaller. We were worried in case all the coal would be sold before it was our turn to be served. After all that time we were only allowed half a hundredweight of coal each. It was very strictly rationed; even so, it was very hard work pushing and pulling that coal home. We searched the rubbish tip, looking for anything that would burn.

Mom was ill for many months. She lost the use of one hand so she started doing knitting and gradually the movement came back into her hand. She slowly recovered, but it was a very scary time. She had always been there for all of us and was never ill. To imagine being without her was totally unthinkable. She had always gone without for us and, indeed, she was the one who held us all altogether.

I soon found another factory job, and another—*and* another. I never stayed in any of the jobs for very long. My aim was to earn as much money as possible before total boredom set in. No factories held any fear for me after the first one. There I had been thrown in at the deep end at fourteen, and all the other jobs were easy compared to that one.

I decided that if I did have a boyfriend he must have red hair like my brothers. I don't know why I had such a thing about red hair! I did meet a boy with the required coloured hair and went out with him several times—and he wanted to get serious; but although I liked his lovely hair, I wasn't that keen on the rest of him! So that relationship soon died a natural death.

When I was nineteen I thought I had *really* met my dream man. I was a very naïve nineteen-year-old and thought, "This is it!" He was twenty-six, nearly six feet tall, good-looking and with beautiful wavy red hair. I only went out with him about three times and I was completely infatuated with him. I didn't know he was a terrible flirt, and when he failed to turn up for a date I thought my heart would break and wept buckets full of tears. It was then that I decided my future role in life would be that of a maiden aunt.

At this time I was working in a factory that made electrical goods. I was working on a conveyor belt that dipped the completed parts into a tank of enamel. There were four of us girls working that conveyor. Two of us filled up racks with the parts. One girl put the racks onto the moving belts that would slowly move into the enamel; then the racks would lift out of the enamel to drain before going into the very large oven to dry. It would then move out of the oven and slowly make its way to the other end of the conveyor where the other girl would take off the parts and sort them into different boxes according to shape and size. The work was still very hot when it reached that end and the girl had to wear thick gloves. It was an enormous machine and all four of us worked very hard.

I didn't mind the hard work. It didn't bother me at all, for by this time I was well used to hard work. Compared to some of the jobs I had flitted through in the past, this one was a doddle.

It made a change to be reasonably happy in a job for once. We were piecework and all the money we earned was pooled between us. That meant we only got paid for the work we actually did. Luckily we all got on with each other and worked well as a team. No one bothered us, or told us what to do. We did the job correctly so there wasn't ever any need for supervision. We were earning more than seven pounds each a week, which was brilliant money, and although men generally earned much more than women in those days (there was no equal pay then), we were earning much more than lots of the men working there. (We weren't silly enough to let on just how much we were earning! There would have been a riot if we had. We always worked much harder than the men anyway.)

Just before lunchtime Friday we would stop putting the work on the conveyor, and by the time we went back to work after lunch the earlier work had gone through the oven which would then be turned off. All four of us would then help to remove the work at the far end. We would then have to get long hooks and reach over into the enormous enamel tank to retrieve all the work, bars and hooks that had fallen into the tank during the week. After we had done that we all found hessian sacks and some string, poked two holes in the sacks, then tied the bags around us to give us some small protection; thus attired, we then went out into the factory yard searching for old and broken palettes and any other rubbish that would burn. We then made a bonfire, and when it was well alight we gathered up all the rakes, bars and hooks we had retrieved from the enamel tank and which were now thickly covered in enamel. We would throw the lot onto the fire and stand back to watch the fire remove the enamel. All four of us had to have a turn at poking the fire to make sure the enamel was all burnt off. We would get red in the face from the fierce heat of the fire.

Although this was a filthy job and there was nowhere at work for us to get cleaned, we didn't mind because it gave us time to stand and have a rest without the continual rushing around. This was part of the job that wasn't piecework: we got a good rate for the work so we didn't lose out. When all the enamel had burned off the equipment, we got long sticks and removed every item from the fire, waited until it had all cooled down, then placed all the things ready in the right order to start work again Monday morning.

We always made sure we spread the job out for most of the afternoon. We didn't want to finish that job too early, just in case we were given another job to do! We couldn't have gone back on the conveyor then, because the oven was shut down for the weekend.

The fumes from reaching into the enamel tank hurt my eyes, making them very sore. I always had two or three styes on my eyes at any one time. As soon as one lot healed, another lot would appear. The styes were a nuisance, but I came to regard them as an occupational hazard.

One day a new girl started work at the factory. Her accent was so much different from our Black Country speech. She was from the South of England. We thought her accent was very posh, so during our tea breaks we would deliberately engage her in conversation, just to hear her "Posh voice." We would then have a go at imitating her voice! When we got to know her better she told us about herself and her family. Her mom had just married a man from our town and the whole family had moved to our area. She told us she had a twenty-year-old brother in the Royal Navy. She said she was sure he would like a girl pen friend and she asked me to write to him. I said, "No thanks, I'm not interested." My friend Ivy was already courting but said she would write to him. She gave the girl her address and thought no more about it. Several days later she was surprised to receive a letter from the boy. She wrote back and they began to correspond quite regularly. She always brought the letters to work for me to read.

One day when I came home for my lunch, mom met me at the door to say there was a letter for *me*. I was amazed, for apart from my birthday presents from my aunt I had never had a letter addressed to me in my life! So, who could it be from? I held the letter in my hand trying to imagine who it came from. I turned it this way and that. I really wanted to open it, but I was savouring the final moment. My family were as curious as me and asked if I had a secret admirer!

It would have had to have been a very secret admirer since I hadn't a clue just who it was from.

The letter, in fact, was from a twenty-year-old sailor named Peter. Unknown to me, my friend had sent my name and address to her pen friend Alec, who had passed it on to *his* best mate. It was a very short and polite letter, asking me to write to him. He came from Aldershot, the same town as his friend; they had grown up in the same street and had been friends since they were little. At fourteen they had joined a training ship together called the *Arethusa*; then, just before their sixteenth birthday, they had joined the navy as boy seamen. They had just returned from a two and a half year foreign commission in the Mediterranean.

I didn't really want a pen friend, especially after I had said that I didn't want to write to the first boy. I had no intention of answering the letter, but then I thought it wouldn't hurt to be polite. So I wrote a short letter back and posted it, not expecting to hear from him again. I thought it wasn't important; we would never meet, so it didn't matter anyway.

I didn't realise just how wrong I was! I received another letter almost by return of post. We wrote to each other quite regularly, and in this way my pen-friendship with Peter began. I soon began to notice just how much we had in common with each other: we liked the same kind of music and we both read a great deal. We were both very shy, too. Although Peter had travelled all over the world and I had never been away from home, it didn't seem to matter. His letters seemed to be telling me he was lonely. That feeling I well understood. He wanted someone to talk to through his letters, and to my amazement I found I was good at writing letters.

Peter is five weeks older than me. He was five feet nine with black hair, and when he sent me a photo I realised he was quite good looking—even though his hair was black and not my favourite red colour! But it wasn't important—we were only pen friends, anyway.

Ivy and I used to take our letters to work, each reading the other's letters. The two other girls must have got really fed up with us both. Our main topic of conversation seemed to be about the two sailors we were writing to—and then one day Panic Stations!

Peter and his friend Alec had some leave and Alec was coming to our town to meet his new stepfather for the first time. It was decided that Peter would spend a few days at Alec's new home. He asked if he could meet me during that time.

Panic Stations again! I had got used to writing to a sailor and didn't actually *want* to meet him. I didn't want to get involved with someone I wouldn't see very often, someone whose home and family were hundreds of miles away from mine. I lived in a small close community and came from a very close family. I had never been anywhere, and the South of England could have been the other side of the world as far as I was concerned.

My friend Ivy and Alec had been writing to each other for some time now, and through their letters had grown very fond of each other. I told Ivy I wasn't interested in meeting the sailors, but she was very keen on meeting Alec. She said Peter was only spending a short time at Alec's home and we could go out as a foursome. So, reluctantly, I agreed.

It was pouring with rain on the evening we had arranged to meet. I was undecided whether to go or not, but I had given my word. I would go just this once, I decided. So Ivy called for me and we set off, both of us feeling very nervous. I was ready to back out at the least excuse. We had had a hard day at work and I was tired. We missed our bus and had to walk more than a mile in the pouring rain. To say that didn't please me at all is a slight understatement. Although I had recently bought a new coat, I decided not to wear it and instead wore a tatty raincoat. My shoes hurt and I grumbled all the way there. I really wasn't in the best of moods. I had the usual styes on both my eyes, too, and didn't bother with any makeup—it would have been a waste of time anyway. In any case, this was going to be the first and last date, so I wasn't really bothered.

We finally reached our destination that was outside a pub in the middle of the town. The two sailors were waiting in the doorway. I think they had been diving in and out of the pub. Perhaps they were as nervous as we were. Alec, by far the most outgoing of all of us, introduced Peter and himself to us. He was just as fair as Peter was dark. Alec was about five feet seven, and slim. He walked with the sailor's gait and was easygoing and jolly. He wore his sailor's cap on the back of his head (quite against naval regulations). Peter, on the other hand, wore his cap exactly one inch above his eyebrows. We seemed to have paired up right, for the other two were much more easygoing than us and were soon chatting away like old friends. The lads turned to go back into the pub and I told them I had never been in a pub in my life and wasn't about to start then. We walked about, still in the pouring rain, and then decided to go into the local cinema. I don't recall the film we watched, but I do know my feet were aching. As soon as we sat down I gently eased my shoes off, breathing a big sigh of relief as I wriggled my toes and settled down to watch the film.

All was well until it was time to go out of the cinema. I felt around with my feet for my shoes but could only find the one. I was too embarrassed to say anything and tried to reach down without anyone noticing. But there was no way I could find my shoe! The others were standing up ready to go, and I finally had to tell them. The lads thought it was a huge joke and told everyone within ten rows to stand up while they searched for my shoe! They climbed over the backs of the seats, going from one row to the next. Alec finally found it! It had been kicked down several rows.

He held it up in the air like a trophy, shouting at the top of his voice that he had found it! I grabbed the shoe from him and ran out of the cinema with it still in my hand. I was too embarrassed to stop to put it on! All four of us left the cinema in a fit of giggles. That episode certainly broke the ice for us all.

Ivy lived in the street at the back of our house, so we finally had to split up, with Peter escorting me and arranging to meet Alec at the bottom of our street later on. We stood at our gate chatting for quite a while, then made arrangements to meet the following evening. When Peter turned to go he made an attempt to plant a kiss on my lips, which I saw coming. I quickly turned my face away so that the kiss landed on my cheek. I didn't intend to let him kiss me on a first date, and told him so in no uncertain terms. Going indoors, all the family were waiting to know how I had got on, and just what Peter was like. I remarked that he was all right, but that he hadn't made much of an impression on me and I didn't intend to see him ever again.

What I certainly didn't know then was when Peter returned to his friend's home that evening he straight away wrote a letter to his mother, telling her he had met his future wife! Just as soon as his mother received the letter she sent him a telegram telling him to go home and take his girlfriend with him. She was alarmed by the speed of it all, and perhaps thought that some hussy had collared her son! Not surprisingly, she wanted to know just what was happening. Peter very wisely didn't tell me he had written that letter to his mother until a long time later. I could have told his mother that nothing was happening! I would have run a mile if I had known about that letter.

At work the next day Ivy asked me if I liked Peter. She wasn't too pleased when I said I wasn't very keen and that I had no intention of keeping the date for that evening. She had finished with her other boyfriend and had grown very fond of Alec and she didn't want her date with him spoilt. She knew Peter didn't know the area and Alec wouldn't leave him on his own, not knowing anyone. She nagged me, saying it was only for three more evenings after which Peter would have gone to spend the rest of his leave with his own family and I needn't ever see him again. I reluctantly agreed to carry on the four-some for the next three days. So we all got to know each other better; we did quite a lot of giggling and had a tolerable time. The other two were now decidedly fond of each other, and though I did get to like Peter, my feelings for him hardly went beyond liking. He didn't even try to kiss me again after that first night when I had told him off.

On the Friday evening we were talking at our front gate when Peter said he wasn't looking forward to the long boring train journey home. I said I would go indoors and find some magazines for him. I told him to wait outside by the gate and I would bring them out to him—and to my great annoyance he followed me into the house! That meant, naturally, that I had to introduce him to my family.

In those days, if a girl took her boyfriend home, it meant she was courting! I knew that—and my family knew that.

So did Peter.

Although I was getting to like Peter, I didn't want to be pressurised into any situation I couldn't get out of. But at that moment there wasn't a lot I could do about it! Anyway, my mom invited him in and made him welcome the way she did for anyone who came to our home. Peter was nervous and wanted a cigarette. He handed his cigarettes round, asking Jessie if she "was having one?" She replied, "No, that's just the way my dress hangs!"

Poor Peter! He was getting the family treatment and he was terribly embarrassed—just as my sister had meant him to be.

I don't think he had ever met a family like mine before.

Everyone fell about laughing, including Peter, and I was very relieved that he had a sense of humour, for he would have been plagued unmercifully by my brothers and sisters if he hadn't. After my family had finished grilling Peter I eventually found the magazines I had promised, and when I walked out to the gate with him I casually asked him what he had thought of my beautiful seventeen-year-old sister.

Up till then no one outside of our family had ever given me a second glance when she was around. After all the years I should have got used to the situation, but it never had got any easier for me. My jealousy was always at the fore, ready and waiting to boil over at the least little thing. Up till then I had made my sister's and my own life a misery. It wasn't her fault she was beautiful and I wasn't. It wasn't her fault either that I had carried a huge chip on my shoulder for seventeen years. My family treated us both equally. It was outsiders who made the comparison between us—or perhaps it was just all in my mind. Whichever it was, I knew it always made both our lives a misery.

I was very surprised and pleased when Peter answered, "She seems like a nice kid!" She was a nice kid! Right! So why, why hadn't I realised that before? Just why did I need a stranger to come into my life and help to pull down the awful walls of jealousy, pain and anger—feelings of envy that had began the moment my sister was born? I felt a wonderful feeling of relief—and happiness! In that instant all of my jealousy disappeared forever. I wanted to run indoors and tell my sister straight away just how I felt. But how could I convince her my feelings were sincere when I had always given her such a hard time?

It was going to be hard work, but if it were going to take the rest of my life, I would do it.

It was a wonderful feeling to know that someone liked me enough to want to continue our pen friendship; it was also a great boost to my ego. I knew though even if nothing ever came from my friendship with Peter, I would be grateful to him always for finding the few right words to release all my pent up anger and frustration—the right words that had finally got through to me. It made me realise he was a very kind person. He would never know just how much it meant to me, and how grateful I would always be.

Saturday morning I found myself thinking of Peter on his long train journey home. I was beginning to realise I was getting to like him much more than I thought would be possible. Although it was very hard for us to converse, he couldn't understand my Black Country dialect at all, and I had a great problem trying to work out his posh King's English voice. It was almost as if we were speaking a different language from each other. The four of us had a great deal of laughter, each of us trying to interpret for one another.

We continued with our letter writing and it was mostly through the letters that we got to know each other a great deal better. Peter had had a very hard life from the age of fifteen when he had joined a training ship. During the training time the boys were not allowed to wear shoes and had to go about their duties barefoot, and were only allowed to wear anything on their feet when they went into town or to Church. If ever they were caught smoking they would be caned. They had to be in bed by nine o'clock. They didn't receive any pocket money at all, and the only time Peter had any money was when his mother sent him a monthly postal order which he spent in one go buying cake from the canteen: as a growing lad he was always hungry.

When he became a boy seaman his pay was eight shillings and nine pence a week. The majority of his pay was banked for him until he became an ordinary seaman. While he was a boy seaman second class he received two shillings a week pocket money which was raised to three shillings and six pence on land; when he was at sea—when he became a boy seaman first class—it was raised to the magnificent sum of five shillings. When he was seventeen and a half he passed the educational tests one and two, which meant he received accelerated promotion six months early and became an ordinary seaman with the huge wage of three pounds a fortnight!

He also told me that once when he returned from three years abroad he decided he would quite like to have a stroll through a beautiful English park, somewhere down the south of England (I won't say where); but, when he reached the gates, there was a huge notice that said: "Strictly no dogs or sailors allowed in this park." Although Peter was a very young man, that notice deeply offended him. He was too young to have seen service during the war, but that notice was displayed only about three or four years after the war ended. Someone responsible for that park had a very short memory.

I enjoyed writing, and found my letters were often ten or twelve pages long. Goodness knows what I found to write about! We were soon writing almost every day, but Peter's letters were never more than a couple of pages long. (I have had plenty of time since those days to know that Peter hates writing letters!) The letters continued for a few weeks and then Peter wrote that he had a weekend leave and was coming to see me, and that he would find somewhere in Birmingham to stay and visit me each day from there.

My home was a good twenty miles from Birmingham, so I didn't really think that was a good idea; also, I couldn't afford to have time off work to be with him. When I told my mom just what he was going to do, she immediately said we couldn't let him stay anywhere else and he could stay with us. It would be very difficult, but not impossible to find room in our home for him. Anyway, my mom said it could be done, so it could be done! We did have a four-bedroom house, and by that time my elder brother and sister had moved into their own homes. My younger brother, his wife and child were still living at our home and waiting in the housing queue until their points had reached the required level to get them a house. There were very few houses being built and though both of my brothers had served their King and Country well during the war, they were both married with a son and daughter before they had collected enough housing points for their council houses. They would have had to wait longer if both of their children had been the same sex, because if the second baby was the same sex as the first, that wouldn't warrant any extra points and therefore no climb up the housing ladder. Four of my mom's five children started their married life living in the family home, and seven of my mom's eleven grandchildren spent their babyhood there. (Thankfully, not all at the same time!)

I adore my own four grandchildren and spend a great deal of time with them, but I wouldn't want them to live with me! I consider that I have quite a lot of time and patience for my grandchildren, but I haven't the patience of Job, which my mom certainly possessed. The Promised Land fit for heroes didn't materialise for working-class people; in fact life was equally as hard, if not harder for many years after the war with rationing still in force, for at least ten years after the war was over. My family had liked Peter the few minutes they had met him and were quite happy for him to stay with us, so I wrote and told him straight away. He was very pleased to accept and said he could make his own way to our house. Nevertheless, I decided to go and meet him in Birmingham. I had been there several times during my childhood, though never on my own. It seems ludicrous now to think that a twenty-year-old, who had been working hard and earning a living for six long years, had never been out anywhere on her own; but that was the way things were in a Black Country family in those days.

I was determined, nevertheless, not only to go to the big city, but to make another first and go into a railway station. We were a very protective family and had always looked out for each other, and both my sister and brother offered to go with me; but this was something I wanted to do by myself and insisted on going alone. I was drilled on where to catch the bus, and where I would have to change buses. Finally, after all the warnings about not speaking to any strangers and being told what to do and what not to do, I set off on my adventure into the big city.

All I could think of was my family telling me not to speak to strangers—but just how was I to find out where to go without asking directions? I wandered up and down different streets feeling very scared until I finally found the station. I didn't know just how long it would take to get there, so I went much too early, arriving at the station at least an hour before the train was due. I stood in a big queue and watched other people putting their pennies into a machine to receive their platform tickets. I didn't even know that I had to have a ticket to go onto the platform, but everyone else was queuing for the tickets so I did the same; but horror of horrors—what if the penny was too thin? Or what if it got stuck in the machine? I was sweating to get things right. I finally managed that hurdle, though going onto the platforms was unnerving: they were crowded and very noisy; and mindful of all the warnings from my family, I was very uneasy. It was quite some time before I managed to find the right platform. I was still much too early for the train from Portsmouth but I didn't mind that and thankfully sat down to wait. I knew it would be a long wait, and Birmingham railway station seemed such a cold and frightening place to me. Now, though, I could relax. I had made it and, more importantly, I had done it on my own!

I sat back watching the trains coming and going, watching people hurrying about their business. They all seemed to know just what they were doing. None of them looked half as scared as I had been. I was so busy watching everyone around me that I almost missed the announcement that the Portsmouth train was arriving! I stood up with the rest of the crowd to watch the train pull in. It was full to overflowing with sailors all waving and hanging out of the windows. The doors opened and out poured hundreds of tall, short, thin, fat, laughing, shouting, waving sailors, good naturally pushing and shoving each other to be first off the train. I searched all the faces until I recognized the one sailor who was neither tall or short, fat or thin, laughing, or shouting. He was waving like mad. We pushed and elbowed our way through the crowds and then, to my own complete amazement, we ran straight into each other's arms. This time I didn't turn my face away when he kissed and hugged me. When I saw him get off that train I immediately knew in a blinding flash that I loved him. This was the one person I would spend the rest of my life with.

This man, I knew, would be the father of my unborn children!

Although I had only met Peter four times and up till then hadn't even kissed him, and while I certainly wasn't an impulsive person, I knew in that instant we would always be together and love each other forever. Although we were both twenty years old, neither of us had loved or had any relationship with anyone else. This wonderful feeling of first love for both of us was really magical.

I forgot all about my dreams of a red headed boyfriend. Peter's hair was very dark but I didn't care. *I loved him and that was that!*

We moved with the crowd out of that station, holding each other tightly, afraid to let go, both of us knowing that something special and wonderful had happened.

We were in love.

Birmingham railway station isn't the most romantic place in the world, but it was the place where we found each other. I was a completely different person walking out of that station from the scared, frightened person who had walked into it. For the first time in my life I was confident, sure of myself, happy and felt ten feet tall holding on to my first and only love. I walked through the streets of Birmingham as if it were an everyday accomplishment, my confidence in myself growing with each step. It was a wonderful experience for me. The inferiority complex I had had all my life was quickly disappearing with each step. This time I had no problem at all finding the right bus stop. We chatted non-stop, laughing and giggling, because we didn't really understand each other's accents. That wasn't important! We could communicate! We could understand the language of love.

We both knew we had so very much to learn about each other. We also knew we had the rest of our lives to find out. The most important thing right then was that we were two people from different parts of the country who, through fate, had found each other; and we both knew we would never ever let go of each other—and we knew that this was for real.

I held Peter's arm as I walked up our street, which was a sign for any nosy neighbours who may have been peering from behind their net curtains that I was courting. The people of the Black Country had some strange and rigid ideas about what was right and wrong, and I well knew that holding a boy's arm meant that a couple were going steady. It was almost considered an engagement. My family could see straight away I was different—and they were happy for me. They were very protective towards me, too. They didn't know anything at all about Peter, and although I was twenty and had grafted hard for six years, I was a complete innocent, knowing nothing at all about life.

My family were fearful for me, not wanting to spoil my new happiness, but at the same time not wanting to see me get hurt. Through my innocence I could have got hurt badly if Peter had been the wrong person for me. But luckily my instinct was right, for he was very much the right person. We had a marvellous weekend which we spent getting to know each other better. Peter bought me a glass-top table from a second-hand shop. The table cost two pounds ten shillings, which was a big chunk out of his money, for it represented almost a week's pay for him. That was the first thing for my bottom drawer. I still have the table which has done many moves with us. I've told our eldest daughter I've bequeathed the table to her, but somehow she isn't overly keen on the idea!

Peter was always generous, bringing chocolates for me and mom, and a box of biscuits for my sisters, and some of his cut-price cigarettes for my brothers. I believe his ration of the cut-price cigarettes was two hundred a week. My brothers soon made short work of the cigarettes. Sunday evening came all too soon. I wanted to go to Birmingham to see Peter back on the train, but he said no, he would rather I didn't, so I walked to the bus stop with him. We both promised to write to each other straight away.

When Peter arrived back on board his ship he told Alec we were getting engaged. His friend was horrified, calling Peter all sorts of names—unprintable here. He said we had only been writing to each other for a few weeks, and we had met less than half a dozen times—which was quite true. He tried his best to talk Peter out of getting engaged, thankfully to no avail. The same thing happened to me when I went back to work on the Monday morning. My friend thought I was crazy.

It was some weeks before I saw Peter again. He couldn't afford the fare to see me because he had to save every penny he had for my engagement ring. It cost him eight pounds and was an awful lot of money in those days. I had given Peter a piece of string for the measurement of my engagement ring. (Fifty years on and I'm twirling that same ring around my finger re-reading this manuscript!) Finally the day came when both Peter and Alec came on a fortnight's leave, and although Alec had said we were crazy to get engaged so soon, he had also bought an engagement ring for Ivy! Peter formally asked my mom if we could get engaged and she gave him a pep talk, telling him that though I hadn't a father I had a mother, so he'd better watch out. My mom may well have been more formidable than any father. Peter told her he loved me and that no harm would ever come to me while he was around. (A promise he has always kept.) My brothers also had a few choice words for Peter, although their message wasn't so finely worded. I believe the gist was that they would both knock his block off if any harm came to me. (They would have done, too!) In spite of all the talks he still stayed, which proved to my family all they wanted to know—that he did love me.

Mom put on a special engagement tea for all four of us. It was a lovely time and both Ivy and myself walked about flashing our rings at the least opportunity.

After a few days at my home I went with Peter to meet his family, an event I certainly wasn't looking forward to. It was the first time in my life I had been on a train! It was quite an adventure for me, especially crossing through London and going on an escalator. I had never done any travelling before, but I knew I was quite safe. Peter had travelled all over the world and he had enough confidence for both of us.

Peter's mom and his brother and sister were very surprised that we had become engaged so soon. Although they didn't say anything, I don't think they were very pleased. It wouldn't have made the slightest difference if they had made any remarks, however. We had already got over the greatest hurdle—convincing my mom, who was a great matriarch. After that anything else was a doddle. We had a pleasant few days at Peter's home and did a lot of walking. We went to the posh area of Aldershot, looking at all the big fancy houses. One particular house I liked the look of was called "Linger Longer," and we promised ourselves that one day when we had our own home we would call it "Linger Longer."

It was marvellous to be introduced to the countryside. We walked for miles down country lanes. Peter showed me places from his childhood. We saw a sign saying "Farnham one mile," so we decided to walk there. We went round in circles for at least eight miles, but we never did reach Farnham. I certainly wasn't used to long walks and I hadn't the right shoes for walking, and when we finally arrived back at Peter's home both my feet were bleeding quite badly. His mom bandaged my feet and gave him a right telling off for getting lost and walking me so far. Although Peter had to go back to his ship at Portsmouth, which is only a few miles from Aldershot, he insisted on coming all the way back on the train with me, staying overnight, then having the long journey back the next day.

We continued to write daily, although now Ivy and I no longer showed our letters to each other. We had some great weekends, still going out as a foursome, and although I didn't drink I would now go into the lounge of a public house. People got to know us and used to plague the lads, saying they were always on weekend leave, and that it wasn't like that in their day.

We used to go to a picture house that was right at the top of the town, then come out of the pictures and go straight into a fish and chip shop next door. We would be laughing and giggling, eating as we walked along until we came down the town to another fish shop. The lady who kept this shop was well over six feet tall, as thin as a rake with her hair tied back into a bun at the back of her head. She had a long thin nose and was the image of Popeye's ladyfriend Olive Oyl! Olive (as we called her) would be busy serving a long queue and wouldn't at first notice us. By the time she did we would have eaten the top layer of our fish and chips (which we had purchased from the first shop) and the salt and vinegar would have been consumed; so Peter and Alec would take our half-eaten snack, go into Olive's shop, walk to the head of the queue and say, "It's all right, we aren't jumping the queue, we're just having the salt and vinegar. Olive wont mind!" The queue would move back to allow them to get to the counter where the salt and vinegar was placed. They would then shout, "Thanks, Olive!" and run out before she had time to realise what they were up to. She would open the flap of the counter, grab a fish scoop and chase after them, shouting, "You cheeky young buggers! It's about time you went back! You're always here with your bloody cheek all the time!"

They would both run like mad! Then, when they were well out of range, they would turn round and answer her back. The people in the queue would be falling about laughing. Early on in the evening, when we were going to the pictures and having to pass the shop, Olive would be there preparing the food ready for the next opening. Peter and Alec would knock on the window to draw her attention and shout: "We'll see you later, Olive! Get plenty of salt and vinegar on the counter!" She always shouted back: "I'll get you two buggars one of these days!" I don't think she really minded their cheek. I don't know if Olive's fish and chips were good or not, having never tasted them; I do know, though, that her salt and vinegar tasted great.

Our main topic of conversation at work was about our sailors. We were working hard and saving money for our weddings. Peter's naval pay was now the massive sum of four pounds, while I was earning over seven pounds a week. He always said he was marrying me for my money! He was allowed every other weekend off. The other weekend he was supposed to be on duty, but that weekend he always gave another sailor ten shillings to do whatever it was he was supposed to do. I never inquired too much about that arrangement. He never got into any trouble, so the other sailor must have well deserved his ten shillings doing a good cover job. Peter was nearly always broke and often hitchhiked to my home, sometimes with just a penny in his pocket. I never knew just how he had the nerve to do that. He would give the people who gave him a lift some of his cheap cigarettes. Sometimes he was home much quicker than he would have been had he come by train. The trouble with that arrangement was I never knew the exact time he would be home. I always made sure he had enough money to go back on the train. My mom always made a pile of lamb sandwiches for him. She would spread cold gravy on the bread—something he had never tasted before and which he thought was great. We introduced him to lots of our Black Country dishes, like pig's tail, pig's trotters, brawn, bacon bits boiled with grey peas. (There's a Black County name we used for the grey peas which modesty forbids me to repeat here.) He thought it very strange that we always had pork pie for Christmas Breakfast.

On the rare occasions when he did have money he would sometimes arrive by coach. I would go into Birmingham and wait at the coach station. When the sailors saw me they always sang, "I'll take you home again Kathleen!" I felt quite chuffed having a coachload of sailors singing to me, but I only ever had eyes for one of them!

The best time of all was when it was foggy on Sunday nights—much too foggy to travel. That meant the lads would have an extra night. There couldn't have been many people about who wanted it to be foggy, but we did. Now, looking back, I cannot think why it was so important to us to have that extra night, for we were never left alone for long, and I had to get up early the next morning for work—so we weren't much better off time wise. We had a full household and the only concession we had was for my family to go to bed earlier to give us some time to ourselves—which they did. But we knew that they were lying awake upstairs, and although we were now engaged there was no hanky panky, and most definitely not in my mom's home! *The very idea was unthinkable!*

We would feel our way through the fog to the police station, which was a couple of miles away. All four of us would be arm in arm. We would be laughing and singing all the way. The police always signed a chit confirming it was impossible to travel, which put the lads into the clear—at least it did most times, though once they were called before the captain who immediately put them both on a charge. They protested and produced the chits from the police, but all to no avail! The captain told them they were seamen and as such should be able to read the weather signs. He said they should have known it was going to be foggy and started out even earlier to beat the fog. He should have realised that ratings wouldn't go back a minute before they had to! Maybe he was having a bad day, or maybe he had never been young.

19

During Peter's summer leave we went to stay with his uncle and aunt in Sussex. I was wary of going because I wasn't very outgoing and didn't like meeting new people. Nevertheless they made me very welcome straight away, especially uncle Bill who was a kind and gentle man. Although I had been introduced to the countryside at Aldershot, this was really something else! It was the loveliest place I had ever seen in my life: the sheer beauty took my breath away. I didn't even know such wonderful places existed. Uncle Bill was the manager or bailiff of this massive out-of-this-world estate (out of my world, anyway). Up till then the only environment I knew was of factories—the smoke, dust and grime of the factory chimneys. The fine manor house had been turned into a retreat for missionaries of all denominations, a place where they could rest and recoup after their long times abroad. It was a beautifully peaceful, happy place. We spent all of our time outdoors walking for miles and never going off the estate at all. We were given the run of the whole place. Sometimes we would just walk around hand in hand, and other times just sit on the haystacks watching the rabbits running around. That really fascinated me—I had never seen rabbits running free before. The only rabbits I had ever seen were the ones mom bought from the market, skinned, then cooked in a huge iron stew pot! That was our special Saturday night treat we enjoyed while listening to *In Town Tonight* on the wireless.

The estate was owned by two titled ladies who were ladies in every way. Often we would meet them on our walks and they would stop and have a chat. They made us very welcome. The property seemed to stretch for miles and miles. Sometimes we would just sit and watch men working in the fields. I had a great feeling of peace, quietness and happiness just sitting there and watching the men going about their work driving the tractors. Other times we would just sit and talk to the many different people of all races and colour. It was all very strange and wonderful to me. Peter's uncle and aunt lived in the lodge that belonged to the estate. It was a large beautiful four-bedroom detached house. It had a great big dining room which, to me, having been used to eating and living in one room, seemed very grand. I had never even been in a detached house before. It was lovely to look out of the many windows, knowing I was enclosed in the grandeur of the countryside.

The estate generated its own electricity, although there was an electricity meter in the house. Uncle Bill used to get a shilling out of his pocket, put it into the meter, twist a handle, and the shilling would drop out of the meter—after which he would put the shilling back into his pocket! He did that every day and seemed to get great amusement from the ritual.

We used to walk around the many acres of greenhouses that uncle Bill lovingly attended. He would pick out fresh fruit for me, and every morning he brought me a beautiful rose. For the first time in my life I was being spoiled and I loved it!

Uncle Bill also had about an acre of land that went with the lodge and was for his own use. All kinds of flowers abounded. I knew the names of none of them; nevertheless, I could (and did) appreciate their beauty. There was a huge plot with every known vegetable on it. Uncle Bill started work very early each morning and would go back home for his breakfast about ten o'clock, and ask auntie May which vegetables she wanted for that day. Food was picked, cooked and eaten inside of one hour—wonderful, fresh, clean food.

They kept chickens, ducks, geese (which I kept clear of), dogs, cats and a very old parrot that swore a great deal of the time and gave wolf whistles that could be quite embarrassing. Although I wasn't used to animals, they didn't bother me too much, except that I have a phobia for cats—I'm terrified of them! They make me sweat and still make me feel cold and shaky. I'll never go into a room if a cat is in there. Peter's uncle and aunt must have thought that very strange! Nevertheless they always made sure the cats were kept well out of my way.

There were apple, plum and pear trees, raspberries and strawberries. Auntie May made jellies, jams, and pies. There were always lovely cooking smells emerging from the large kitchen.

There was such a great deal of new and wonderful things for me to learn about, to see, to touch, to smell—wonderful new joys I had never in my life experienced: the musical dawn chorus of all the many different birds, cows and sheep grazing in the fields, the squirrels running around, the barking of foxes, the tractors working the land, the harvest being gathered in.

Most of all, though, I loved the fantastic hues, shades, and colours of the countryside. I enjoyed the quiet, the unrushed atmosphere of the whole place. It was all so very different from my hectic and hard life in the Black Country.

I got on very well with Peter's uncle and aunt—so much so that uncle Bill told Peter that if he ever let me down in any way, he would not be welcome there again! I believe he well knew there was no fear of that happening. It was good to know I had made a hit, although they must have realised straight away I knew absolutely nothing about the countryside and was very eager and happy to learn. They took great pleasure in showing me the wonders of their environment—Uncle Bill, especially, who was a real old-fashioned born and bred countryman. He really took me under his wing, explaining everything to me in great detail. He was a good teacher and I an eager pupil. It was a marvellous introduction to the countryside. I never wanted that fantastic holiday to end.

Sussex, to me, was a beautiful place, and inspired in me the great love of the countryside I have ever since had, and which I still have for my beautiful adopted County of Shropshire.

20

Peter was seventeen and a half when he joined the regular navy. At that time he had to sign on until he was twenty-five. There was no getting out of it, even if he wanted to. It seems strange to me that young lads had to sign away such a large part of their lives. But he was always happy in the navy and had intended to make it his career until we met, when he quickly lost interest in the navy. I wouldn't have minded a long engagement and was quite happy to wait until he was demobbed before getting married. But he felt otherwise and was eager for us to get married as soon as possible. In fact, it was only lack of money that stopped us getting married much sooner. He had been left some money from a great uncle—money he couldn't receive until he was twenty-one. It amounted to just over a hundred pounds, which was a great deal of money then. Before he met me he had always intended to buy a fast motorbike with that money. But he said a marriage license only cost seven shillings and six pence, so he must have thought he had a better deal with me. His money was put to much better use, anyway, for a motorbike would have deteriorated and depreciated eventually, whereas I improved with age and have lasted much longer than any bike! I was saving every penny I could and was now paying board for my keep which left me with more money to save. (In the Black Country it was then usual to hand over your unopened pay packet to your mom until your twenty-first birthday.) I was twenty and it was my mom who suggested I should now pay board. I forget just how much it was, but it enabled me to save much more.

Peter's legacy came through three months after his twenty-first birthday. The banns were read and we arranged to get married on the 24th of March 1951. We had only known each other for eleven months and been engaged for eight months. During that time we hadn't spent a great deal of time together, for we did most of our courting by letters. Even though the war had been over for six years, food was still rationed. Mom's sisters (the aunts) were great: they all did the baking and cooking and shared all the catering arrangements between them, using their own rations. They all supplied the crockery and cutlery and made a brilliant job of it. My wedding dress cost seven pounds. (One week's wages!)

Peter's mother, brother and small niece came to the wedding, staying at our home which was already packed. My mom somehow sorted out the sleeping arrangements, I don't remember just how, but if she said it could be done, then it could be done. Peter, his brother, and my two brothers went out on the booze on his stag night. They were all legless! Somehow my brothers managed to get to my sister's home where they borrowed my niece's pram. They put Peter across the pram and they took it in turns to wheel him home, although they weren't in much better condition than he was. Peter's mother wasn't amused, to put it lightly. I think she thought my brothers were leading him astray, never mind that her elder son was just as drunk as they were. She must have wondered just what sort of family he was marrying into. I was furious with both my brothers and with Peter, and in fact had my first row with him. Or rather, it would have been a row if he hadn't been too drunk to understand. The row was one sided, naturally, but I know I really let rip!

The house, as I said, was full to overflowing. Everyone was uptight and ready to explode at the least wrong word. It wasn't a good atmosphere. I didn't think there was any chance that Peter or my brothers would be sober by the next day. Peter's mother was stony faced, too, which certainly didn't help matters any. I said there would be no wedding the next day, but my mom smoothed things over, making gallons of tea and coffee. Peter was staying that night at my sister's house. He was finally put back in (or rather on!) the pram and wheeled round there. Fortunately it was only a couple of streets away.

My sister came round to see me the next morning and reported that Peter was fine, apart from walking up and down, wearing out her carpet and shaking from the effects of a powerful hangover. She had poured large quantities of coffee into him. She had also gone to the off-licence and bought him a bottle of beer—a family ale. (I don't know if she was trying to tell us something, but, like all my family, my sister had a great sense of humour.) The beer was to calm him down—something about the hair of the dog!

It was Easter Saturday, a very busy day for weddings. Lots of people had planned their weddings before April so they could claim back income tax. That didn't apply to us, for Peter certainly didn't earn enough money to pay tax—it just happened that that was the time his leave was due. Although my upbringing had taught me to be very careful with money, I decided just for this one day I was going to be extravagant and spend, spend, spend! My dress was beautiful. Margaret and Peter's small niece were bridesmaids and my nephew was my pageboy, dressed of course in a sailor suit. We paid to have the bells ringing, and the choir sang at a cost of a shilling for each member of the choir. The wedding cake was two-tiered and cost us all a good many food points. Although the wedding had cost us a great deal of money, I didn't think it would have been much of a wedding without all the trimmings; and anyway, I wanted it to be just right for my mom's sake.

My elder brother Eric gave me away. The wedding was the last one of the day and when we arrived at the church someone came out waving like mad. I thought for one horrible moment that Peter hadn't sobered up enough to be at the church, but it turned out the weddings had been running late all day and the one in front of ours was only half way through! All our guests were standing around outside the church. It was a bitterly cold and windy day and they were all shivering with the cold. One of my cousins (the one I used to have fights with when we were children) put her fur cape around my shoulders. (Either she had forgotten about our fights or she had forgiven me by then.) The driver was told to drive round and round the church until someone came out to give him the all clear. We finally arrived in the church nearly half an hour later than the time our wedding was booked for. By this time Peter was a bundle of nerves, though strangely enough I was quite calm.

It was a beautiful service with the bells ringing and the choir singing—well worth all our hard work and hard-earned money. I held my brother's arm and the organ started to play *Here comes the bride!* Everyone stood up. I walked down the aisle and, for the first time in my whole life, I was the centre of attention. Everyone gave me smiles as I walked past. I looked for, and caught my mom's eye. We gave each other a smile that spoke volumes and was especially reserved just for my mom and me.

Peter was shaking like a leaf! He mumbled his vows which hardly anyone heard. I made my vows loud and clear!

We held the reception in an upstairs room at a public house. Peter had ordered several barrels of beer and he had put both of my brothers in charge of distributing the drinks. Knowing my brothers, I thought that was a crazy idea, but he assured me they would be so busy serving everyone else they wouldn't have time to drink much themselves. I was very anxious, though. I didn't want anything to spoil the day, and certainly didn't want a repeat of the night before.

But my brothers were marvellous! Neither of them had more than half a pint of beer. It must have been torture to them to serve beer all night without serving themselves! That was a great sacrifice they made on my behalf and one I very much appreciated. Their great restraint showed me just how much they loved me! Mind you, it could also have meant my mom had had a quiet word with them beforehand and had lain down the law. Whatever the reason I was grateful to them. Although both of my brothers were married men with young families, they had great respect for mom and wouldn't do anything to upset her or me.

It was a lovely "Do" and a good time was had by all! Everyone was on his or her best behaviour. There was one incident, however, when a gatecrasher managed to reach the top of the stairs without anyone noticing. He tried to move into the room but Eric went over to him and quietly told him he had the option of either turning round and walking back down the stairs, or he, Eric, would personally throw him down the stairs. (He would have, too, and without a second thought!) The would-be gatecrasher got the message and thought it prudent to make a quick exit. Several of Peter's naval friends came to the wedding. My aunts made a great fuss of them and they in turn escorted my aunts all day long. The aunts lapped up all the attention, of course.

I changed out of my wedding dress into my trousseau (which I had bought from Bilston market), and, carrying my dress over my arm, Peter and I left the reception before anyone else to walk the couple of miles home. No one in our family had cars in those days.

We were alone in the house for perhaps an hour before everyone else turned up and, although we lived in a four-bedroom house, it was going to be quite crowded with mom, Margaret, my brother Bernard and his wife and child, Peter's mom, brother and niece and Peter and I.

I do remember that mom gave us her bedroom for that first night, but having both my mom and my mother-in-law sleeping in the next bedroom hardly made a good start to our married life! The next day we were going on honeymoon. Everyone thought that was great, for not many people actually went away on their honeymoon, and as far as I know I was the only one in our family that had ever done so. Peter had made all the arrangements for our journey to Bournemouth. His sister and her husband had been there and had given the place the okay, so, accompanied by Peter's family, we caught the train to London.

At long last we were alone! There were only a few hundred passengers on the train, but we weren't too bothered about them for we only had eyes for each other. It was a very long, tiring journey, and it was ten o'clock at night before the train pulled into Bournemouth.

We hadn't a clue how to reach the digs; so tired, cold and hungry, we decided to go mad and treat ourselves to a taxi. There was only the one taxi and a young couple were just getting into it.

The taxi driver asked us where we wanted to go and then said we could all get into the cab. So we all had to huddle together! The driver said he would drop the other couple off first, which he did, after which we were driven for miles and miles. I was beginning to think we would never reach our destination, but finally we did. The fare was enormous—quite a large chunk out of our spending money.

The digs were in a council house. It was a small house with only the one spare bedroom the woman let to supplement her income. She was very angry because she had had to wait up for us and she lost no time telling us either. She grudgingly gave us something to eat and then showed us up to our room, still grumbling. It was a grubby little room, but we were too tired and past caring. At long last we were alone, tired out, cold and still hungry—and so we began our honeymoon.

After breakfast the next morning we decided to go for a walk. We walked down the street and turned a corner, hoping to see the sea; instead—surprise, surprise! —we didn't see the sea but the railway station. In fact, the house we were staying in was only a few hundred yards from the station and throughout our stay there we could hear the trains thundering up and down. Luckily—for him rather than us—we didn't see that taxi driver again!

Peter had paid for us to stay there for ten days so we had to stick it out. Fortunately the weather changed and it became quite warm. We were able to walk for miles and were out every day climbing the cliffs. Peter wore his naval uniform. He kept all his naval papers, his leave pass and our money in the band inside of his cap for safekeeping. We walked on the cliffs for a long time and then sat down. Peter put his cap on the ground and after a while we decided to carry on walking. We had gone quite a way before we realised he had left his cap behind on the cliffs!

We ran back, but everything had disappeared! We were in a terrible state! Even our return tickets were inside the cap. It was a disaster for us, but for all that Peter was more worried that the police would pick him up and arrest him for being improperly dressed without his cap!

We searched those cliffs for hours without any results, until finally we knew we would have to face the music and report the loss to the police. If they decided to arrest Peter for being improperly dressed, there wasn't a lot we could do about it.

So in we went expecting the worst. We hadn't had much joy at Bournemouth up till then. We explained the situation and we were taken into a room where, to our great surprise, was Peter's cap—our money, papers and tickets still intact!

When the police sergeant realised we were on honeymoon, Peter didn't even get a telling off—although he did take the mickey, just a little. We were so relieved that everything had turned out right that we didn't mind the sergeant's mickey taking! We asked who had found the cap but the police said the person didn't want to leave his name. Whoever it was we were very grateful to him. His kindness had helped us to forget, though not forgive the taxi driver and the landlady.

Before we left the lodgings the landlady told us she had a cot and would put it in the bedroom for us the next year. I thought thanks, but no thanks!

Peter came the long journey home with me, and then had to make the journey back to Portsmouth the next day, leaving me to start married life on my own.

Everything slotted back into place at home, and at work on the Monday morning everything was just the same as before.

Had I dreamt I had got married and been on honeymoon? I was doing the same lucrative, soul destroying, boring job as before, and going home in the evenings to mom and my brother and sister, but with no husband in sight. Yet I wore a plain gold ring on my finger. So I *was* married, wasn't I?

Anyway, we *did* have a lovely wedding. We've lived happily ever after, although we've had our fair share of hardships. We've climbed many long and hard hills and always come down them together.

Hopefully, now, I've got the writing bug that will lead to another story.

Or even stories, who knows?

About the Author

Kathleen Hann was born into a poor working-class family in the Black Country during the depression of the nineteen thirties. She was a clever child at a time when it wasn't thought poor children could be clever, when ridicule was the only way the mediocre teachers knew how to deal with the situation. In *Tell it as it Was* she has written a book to make one laugh and cry as she revisits her past and evokes many of the outrageous and picaresque characters of her childhood, her youth and early womanhood.

She was one of a hundred people in Shropshire chosen by the BBC to appear on the programme, *The Century Speaks*, in which the BBC called for people to give their views on Shropshire. Her book is living history, experienced in the raw and tested on the pulses of a real participant whose vision of those times, while sympathetic, sincere and humorous, is never coloured by rose-tinted lenses. She has not given us a dry treatise of social history, but a slice of life that will forever remain with the reader.

0-595-22790-2

Printed in the United Kingdom
by Lightning Source UK Ltd.
106158UKS00001B/253-261